SCHOOL SPIRITS

Volume 1

College Ghost Stories
of the East & Midwest

Mark Marimen

Printed in the United States of America

02 01 00 99 98   5 4 3 2 1

ISBN 1-882376-61-7

Cover photograph by Troy Taylor.
Cover design by Adventures with Nature.

Thunder Bay Press
Holt, Michigan

Other titles in the Thunder Bay Press *Tales of the Supernatural* series:
  Hoosier Hauntings
  Chicagoland Ghosts
  Haunts of the Upper Great Lakes
  Michigan Haunts and Hauntings
  Haunted Indiana

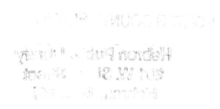

CONTENTS

Other Books by Mark Marimen

Haunted Indiana

Foreword

The English language has plenty of names for it. Goose bumps. The jitters. The willies. However you choose to name it, we are all familiar with the feeling, that delicious and terrifying sensation that creeps over us at odd moments, often just when we least expect it. It is that perception that slithers out from the corners of our psyche when the moon hides behind the clouds just as we happen to pass that old country cemetery. It is that fluttering sensation in the belly when something that we desperately hope is a branch scrapes across our windowpane in the dead of night.

Whenever or however it comes, none among us can completely escape the primal fear that sneaks up to wrap itself around us like a shroud, overriding our conscious sense and letting us know that that there is something waiting out there in the darkness, perhaps waiting for us. It is a fear as old as humanity itself.

For some, it is the stuff of nightmares and as such is to be avoided. Ironically, for the rest of us it is a feeling to be cultivated and enjoyed. In any case, it is a sensation beyond explanation, or even rationality itself. With any luck at all, it might be a great deal of fun.

Time and again, as I have been researching this book, friends have asked me why college ghostlore seems to be so plentiful on campuses across our country. While there may be many reasons for this abundance, I believe that it is partly due to the nature of ghostlore itself, and in large part due to the meaning of those precious college years for many of us.

College is, for most young people, a turning point in life, a coming of age when things of childhood are put away and the pursuit of adult enlightenment and experiences becomes a primary goal. It is a period of putting to death old notions and beliefs and replacing them with a rational view of life. Reason and knowledge become the lenses through which we view our human experience and a cognitive understanding of the universe becomes a seemingly attainable goal. In the process, myth and tradition fade quickly as they are exposed to the harsh brilliance of academic wisdom.

Nevertheless, somewhere in this process of putting away our childhood myths, something precious may be lost—something of our youthful naiveté regarding the world. We lose some of the mystery and wonder of life. In this way college may be a time of knowledge gained, but innocence lost.

Still, for most of us, something of the old remains, a hunger for those elements of life that lie just outside the domain of our human understanding. We hold on to the undeniable realization that despite our vast comprehension of the universe, there still are some things beyond our intellectual grasp. It is the wonderful awareness that outside the light of our technological wisdom, there is still a darkness. And who knows but that in that darkness there may lurk things old and strange and not quite dead?

This is the realm of ghostlore. Perhaps college ghostlore and legends serve an invaluable role on the campuses where they reside. Perhaps they serve as a counterbalance to the academic knowledge and pursuits that so dominate college life. They may exist for the very purpose of reminding us that no amount of understanding will ever rid us of that deliciously frightful feeling that creeps over us at odd moments, when the goose bumps return and the primal fear of the dark and what lies there wraps itself around us.

Within this realm lies this volume of stories.

It never fails to distress me, when searching for collections of ghostlore at my local bookseller, to find such volumes in sections categorized as "New Age Books" or "Metaphysics." To link venerable old ghost stories with such half-baked theologies and philosophical absurdities as books on witchcraft or crystal healing is to denigrate the stories told, and to misunderstand the very nature of ghostlore.

Ghostlore, (including the narratives contained within these pages) is not meant to explain the nature of our universe. These tales of phantoms and ghosts will admittedly shed little light on the nature of human existence, nor will they make any profound theological statement regarding our mortality. They simply serve as a reminder that no matter how great our understanding or comprehension, there will gratefully always be dark concerns of existence, where specters may lurk, and where life still has its wonder and innocence.

Please be warned: if it is great parapsychological truth or deep philosophy that you seek, you might well look elsewhere. However, if you simply wish to slip away from the harsh light of reality for a time to enjoy the delicious, terrible knowledge that there is a darkness out there, and in that darkness there might be things unquiet and undead, then read on.

— Mark Marimen

Note

In the writing of this book, careful attention has been given to collecting legends that in many instances have been told for generations. In some cases, scenes have been recreated in the telling of these old legends that might not reflect historical events. The author makes no claim as to the exact historical authenticity of any of the legends represented in this book. Additionally, some of those who have chosen to tell their stories in this book have requested that their names be changed to protect their privacy. In these cases, an asterisk (*) follows the name the first time it is mentioned.

Dedication

Dedicating a book is truly a difficult task. There are so many who deserve this dedication.

First of all, this book is dedicated once again to Jane and Abby. You are the greatest gifts that God has ever shared with me and next only to God, my life is all about you.

This book is also dedicated to "the guys," a circle of friends that has given my life joy and humor.

This book is further dedicated to my family—Mom and Dad, Jay, Claudia, and their families. I love you all.

Finally, this book is dedicated to the memory of Beth Scott, an author whose books started me on this quest and whose words of encouragement made me believe it was possible.

"The crypt door yawns, and the denizens of the grave beckon. The midnight hour has arrived. Come forward and join us."
— John Chilcraft

Acknowledgments

As Theodore Roosevelt once remarked, "I use not only all the brains God gave me, but all the brains I can borrow as well."

This book is the result, not only of my own efforts, but also of the work and generous help of a great many people. Without their support and effort, it could not have been accomplished.

I wish to thank first Mrs. Patty Wilkins and Mrs. Joyce Dudeck, who helped enormously with the proofreading and editing of this manuscript, as well as incredible general support.

Many thanks to Maureen MacLaughlin and Loretta Crum, my editors at Thunder Bay Press, for their help and kindness in making this project a reality. You have helped make my dream come true and I am grateful.

Thanks are due to the many people I have worked with at the colleges and universities across Midwest and East, who have helped in this project. A special note of thanks is due to Michael Adams of Simpson College, for going above and beyond the call of duty in helping me. Thanks also to those authors who have allowed me to use their material in this work, especially Mark Nesbitt and my dear friends Chris Woodyard and Troy Taylor.

Thanks to Steve Conger, who played an inadvertent part in having this work published, and to Larry Wirtz, information director for the Hoosier Folklore Project, for his aid as well.

Many thanks to Wilfred Wilkins and Commander Jacob P. Wilkins for their contributions to the work on the Battle of Gettysburg.

Finally, I wish to thank a man who is my hero in the field of ghost writing: J. Michael Norman, for writing the introduction to this book. To have my name linked to his is an honor.

Introduction

By asking me to write a few words of introduction to what promises to be a dandy collection of collegiate ghost stories, author Mark Marimen has allowed me to combine two of my adult pursuits—American ghost stories and college teaching. But he might not know that, try as I might, I have been unable to verify with any certainty the presence of restless spirits on my own small Wisconsin campus. Oh, there are plenty of anecdotes and rumors of ghostly sightings at my school, but I've come to believe that the tales are the product of wishful thinking and late-night student parties. Perhaps a student's "coming of age" that Marimen speaks of in his foreword includes a need to see a ghost. Thus they hanker for their own experiences with a spectral professor or blonde, willowy (and quite dead!) co-ed moaning from atop the campus carillon tower.

It's pretty embarrassing, let me tell you, for an individual who has co-authored four books of ghost stories to admit a total absence of revenants at the place where he spends most days of the year. But it's not for want of trying to oblige public expectations.

Each October, with the regularity of a mantel clock chiming in the parlor of the quintessential haunted mansion, eager reporters from the campus weekly knock on my office door to inquire as to whether I know of any ghosts hereabouts. In particular they inquire after South Hall, a four-story brick edifice built in the "normal-school style" and dating back to the 1890s. Until a remodeling a few years ago, it creaked with age—sagging roof, drafty windows, dimly-lit staircases, high ceilings, and an unreliable electrical system. If any building on campus ought to be haunted, some students and staff reasoned, it should be South Hall. It is also the building that has housed the student newspaper offices for many years. So you see, after all those late nights bent over layout tables, typewriters and computers, satiated with stale pizza and flat soft drinks, young scribes looking for their first ghost story might well imagine that phantoms lurked just outside their newspaper office door.

I oblige them by listening to their stories of scurried steps at the midnight hour, inexplicable banging about on the floor above their offices, and swiftly passing shadows in the hallways. When they finish, I tell them all I know of the building's ghost history, which is not much. Alas, there have not been, to my knowledge, any reliable sightings of spectral collegians in the building, though I remain open to the prospect. Many of their experiences, I say to the student reporters, can be attributed to the bats which once inundated the place. I know because I have ducked a few during class lectures. And, being nocturnal mammals, bats would naturally be more active at night. Those are probably the shadows they see and the crashes they hear. The footsteps may have been the squirrels which sometimes found refuge in the attic storeroom.

This leads me to an important point: it is always necessary to eliminate any natural, mechanical or human explanation for hauntings. College students, not unlike the general populace, are sometimes all too willing to accept the supernatural as an explanation without adequately exploring other alternatives. If one wants to create a fictional tale of terror, then it's perfectly fine to avoid the mundane rationale, but to investigate "real" ghost stories, a healthy dose of skepticism is never out of order. Besides, a thorough investigation can lead one down the most exciting avenue of all—the discovery of an event for which there is no worldly explanation. As Sherlock Holmes put it, "When one has eliminated the impossible, whatever remains, however improbable, must be the truth."

Getting at the truth takes some time. For instance, I have been told two sketchy stories of ghost sightings on campus. One involves an old house which was used for art department offices and stood where a new fine arts building is located. It seems something scared the wits out of one of those art teachers late one night. I've also been told this person refused to ever speak of the incident. I have not been able to track down this reluctant pedagogue, but I hope one day to hear the entire story. I am patient. A second anecdote concerns a flamboyant former theater professor whose ghost has been seen in the theater he designed and was able to enjoy for only a year before his untimely death in the mid-1970s. A few, brief secondhand stories of his occasional sighting in the stage wings are all I've heard, and they may only be the product of imaginative theater artists. But again, I'm open to the possibilities.

All of this is what keeps me interested in American ghost stories. That, plus the occasional intriguing telephone call. Recently I heard from a man whose sister lives near Milwaukee. She had told him about some odd goings-on there, but he didn't believe her until his recent visit. He told me he had never been so scared in his life as during that visit when all manner of sounds and shadows disturbed his sleep. The skeptic in many of us would dismiss all this as a too-real nightmare, and perhaps it is. But my informant is finishing his graduate degree in counseling psychology, has no former interest in the supernatural, and even counted himself among the confirmed disbelievers of the world. Even so, one visit to his sister's house has persuaded him to reconsider his position. Now those are the witnesses I really appreciate hearing from. I plan to interview him in the near future.

Mark Marimen has gathered good, solid information about collegiate hauntings and shaped them into some wonderfully intriguing ghost stories from some of America's best-known college campuses. From West Point, to the University of Notre Dame, Kansas State University, and beyond, Mark has managed to pull together virtually all that is known about the ghosts on these campuses. I especially like the way he places each ghost story in a historical context so we learn more about each campus than whether or not long-gone profs go bump in the night. Some are well-known tales (such as those from West Point), while others originate at small schools (Simpson College) not known for their spectral history. I recommend all of them to the reader eager for a chill or two. Best of all, this seems to be the beginning of a series. I look forward to reading every one of them. Happy hauntings!

— *J. Michael Norman*
June 1998

1
The Ghost of College Hall
Simpson College
Indianola, Iowa

What beckoning ghost along the moonlight shade
Invites my steps, and points to yonder glade?
Alexander Pope: *To the Memory of an Unfortunate Lady*

The moon drifts listlessly across the midnight sky, its pallid light filtering gently down through the maple trees lining the walkway. A cool autumn breeze drives the fallen leaves as they skitter across the yard before the ancient brick building. Seeing the structure in such a background, it is not hard to imagine it as a setting for ghost stories. If one looks closely enough at the building itself, it is not hard to imagine, in the Gothic third floor window, the face of a girl staring silently down on the scene below. It is a face devoid of expression or any hint of life itself. It is the face of girl, long dead, whose presence is a reminder of a long-ago tragedy. Her spirit, it is said, silently prowls the corridors of College Hall.

Today, newly renovated and refurbished, College Hall sits serenely on the campus of Simpson College in Indianola, Iowa. A small Methodist-related college just south of Des Moines, Simpson College was founded in 1860 as the Indianola Male and Female Seminary. Though remaining a small liberal arts college, Simpson can boast of a 130-year record of providing sound educational, spiritual and social opportunities for its many alumni.

Among Simpson's graduates was the noted nineteenth-century scientist and agriculturist George Washington Carver, who spent what he later described as a "golden year" at Simpson studying art before moving on to pursue his love of agriculture.

Starting with one building, the school quickly outgrew its single structure, and in 1869 built what became known as the "Old Chapel." Large and expansive for its time, Old Chapel was a massive three-story brick building when completed. High ceilings graced the interior, along with hardwood floors, a large watch tower attached to one side, and a sweeping open staircase just inside the main entrance. Although adding to the majestic beauty of the building, this staircase was fated to play a key role in the legend attached to Old Chapel.

Through the years, Old Chapel was utilized by Simpson College for a variety of purposes. In addition to serving as the chapel for the school, the structure was also used as a library, a classroom facility, and a music conservatory.

College Hall stands on the campus of Simpson College, Indianola, Iowa. A young coed who fell to her death in a stairwell in 1935 is rumored to haunt this building.

Photo: Simpson College Archives

With the passing of time, Old Chapel became the central edifice of the campus, from which all other buildings that eventually rose around it took their form. Today, as when it was first constructed, the building is elegant and beautiful, a graceful reminder of a more genteel era.

It is both interesting and ironic that so noble a building should also, through the years, attract tales of a distinctly tragic and foreboding nature. In its 128-year history, any number of tragic deaths are rumored to have occurred at Old Chapel.

According to college lore, the first person to lose his life at Old Chapel was a young male student who, in the latter days of the nineteenth century, hanged himself from the bell tower after a failed romance. According to the old stories told at Simpson, friends of the ill-fated youth often saw his morose spirit wandering the halls of the building after his death.

In 1924, a young woman was said to have ended her life in the same way in the bell tower, and students point to a memorial passage placed before the girl's picture in that year's college yearbook as proof of the tale. The legends are further enriched by the addition of a rumor that still another young woman is said to have hanged herself by the ornate chandelier that hangs before the third floor window. This purported incident is given credit for the fact that the chandelier in question has been seen to sway at odd moments for no apparent reason.

Verification for most of these incidents is sketchy at best. At least one college historian has voiced his opinion that the stories of students hanging themselves in the bell tower are fictitious anecdotes stemming from an occasion, many years ago, when students hanged the effigy of an unlucky professor from the tower. Indeed, those who know the history of Simpson seem to write off these legends as nothing more than the type of fictitious folklore commonplace on college campuses.

Of one tragic death associated with Old Chapel, however, there can be no debate. Her name was Mildred Hedges, and she came to Simpson in the fall of 1934 to begin her college studies as a home economics major. She was a tall, sturdy-looking girl with brown hair that hung down to her shoulders. Like so many other nameless college freshmen, her first months at Simpson were satisfying if unremarkable. Indeed, she might have spent her entire college career at Simpson in comparative anonymity had not fate taken a cruel hand.

May 6, 1935, began like any other day for Mildred Hedges. The Iowa landscape had shaken off the last vestiges of winter and spring was in the air. Perhaps Mildred, like many college students during that time of year, was looking forward to finishing the spring term in a month and returning home to Scranton, Iowa, for the summer break. It was a vacation she would never get to enjoy.

That morning Mildred attended sewing class, a mandatory freshman offering for home economics majors, held on the third floor of Old Chapel. At 11:55 A.M., class was dismissed and Mildred, along with four or five of her classmates and their instructor, headed toward the large open stairway. In the years to come, there would be much speculation about what happened next.

Perhaps it was the large load of books Mildred held in her right arm that threw her off balance. Perhaps her shoe caught in the hem of the long pleated skirt she wore. Perhaps she simply missed a step. In

Photo: Mark Marimen

The stairwell inside College Hall where Mildred Hedges met her untimely death. Her spirit is said to haunt the building at night.

any case, Mildred suddenly pitched forward over the low banister of the stairwell. Before any of those around her could intervene, Mildred fell headlong down the eighteen-foot drop from the third floor to the first. Perhaps she might have survived the fall with only a broken leg if her head had not hit a table that stood before the main doors in the entryway.

Mildred Hedges never regained consciousness. She died four hours later at Methodist Hospital in Des Moines. A few days later, with the entire campus in mourning, over two hundred of her classmates, neighbors, and friends filed past her casket, surrounded by flowers in the sitting room of her parents' farmhouse in Scranton. The next day her body was quietly laid to rest in a small cemetery nearby.

In other circumstances, this might have been a sad but final chapter in the life of a young girl. Other than a memorial line next to her photograph in the college yearbook and the melancholy recollection of friends, all memory of Mildred Hedges might well have passed into the misty recess of time. But this was not to be the case.

What happened next is perhaps best described by Simpson College Historian Joseph W. Walt, who recently wrote in his history of Simpson, *Beneath the Whispering Maples*:

> Soon a kind of mythology began to grow up around this tragic accident. Some years later people were hearing reports that on late nights— moonless nights to be sure—sounds of a ghost could be heard in the ancient building. Thus was created the legend of the ghost of Old Chapel, still believed by those who want to believe. One cannot escape the feeling that somehow, poor Mildred Hedges deserved a quieter, more decorous immortality.

Perhaps, as Dr. Walt notes, Mildred Hedges did deserve the more "decorous immortality" denied her. However, in the succeeding years, rumors of her ghostly presence at Old Chapel have continued and flourished.

Some of the occurrences might be passed off by skeptics as "mere coincidence" or the common nuisances inherent in old buildings. To others, the strange occurrences they have encountered at Old Chapel are harder to explain. Those present in the building, particularly after dark, have reported hearing doors shut when no one was in the area, and a gentle swishing sound, as if someone wearing a long skirt were

..ng through empty hallways. Lights frequently flicker, particu-
.arly on the third floor, despite the fact that the electrical system has
been checked numerous times and undergone recent renovation.

Other accounts of encounters with the spirit abound. Frequently,
janitorial workers are said to report finding lights turned on in rooms
where they had been turned off and the building had been vacant. Still
other stories are of an even more distinct and eerie nature. Phantom
footsteps are said to traverse the upstairs hallway heading toward the
main staircase. Crashes, as if something heavy has dropped from a
great height, have been heard in the entranceway. Cold spots can be
felt in the building after dark, even on the hottest of summer nights.

One of the strangest legends that has sprung up around the death
of Mildred Hedges is that, after her terrible accident, her blood stained
the steps of Old Chapel near where her body had landed. Further, the
story suggests that after her death, staff found that no amount of cleaning, sanding, or refinishing was able to remove this grotesque memorial to the hapless girl's death.

It is true that for many years, a dark red stain was visible on the
stairs leading up from the main entrance of the building. Campus officials have protested that the stain was merely the result of a paint
spill from years before, but in the collective mind of the student population, this evidence only solidified the ghostly legend of the place.

By 1980, Old Chapel was showing the wear of her 111-year service to the college. With a crumbling foundation and in need of extensive renovation, the board of trustees at one point voted to demol-
ish the structure. Renovation, it was thought, would cost far more
than the building of a new, modern facility. However, just as demoli-
tion was set to begin, the building was saved.

Two members of the board of trustees gained the building a "stay
of execution" while they attempted to raise the funds necessary for
renovation through alumni donations. After the building sat empty
and abandoned for some months, the necessary money was procured
and the renovations began.

Even with the building left vacant and securely locked, the phenomena at Old Chapel are said to have continued. On dark nights
those passing by the aged structure are said to have noticed mysteri-

ous lights going from one window to another despite the building's vacancy. Security police were more than once called to the place after witnesses reported seeing movement in an upstairs window and strange sounds emanating from within the walls of Old Chapel. Invariably, a thorough check of the building found it devoid of human inhabitants.

In 1986, the building was reopened and renamed "College Hall." Newly refurbished and redecorated, the building now serves as offices for the Financial Aid and Admissions Departments, as well as a reception area and small museum. However, even these improvements have failed to rid the building of it spectral presence.

One member of the maintenance staff was recently quoted in the local press as saying that she knew that strange things went on there "all the time." The staff member related that she and her coworkers constantly saw things that were "inexplicable" throughout the building. Lights turned themselves off and on, fire alarms went off for no reason, and doors that had been left open were found locked from the inside with no other exit possible.

If indeed the cleaning staff does routinely confront such strange occurrences, they might at least take comfort in the fact that they are not alone. In 1990, a security guard was reportedly badly frightened after meeting a "translucent woman" in a dark corridor one night. Shaken, the man left the building, returning a few hours later with fellow officers to search the area. No one was found.

Several years ago, a maintenance worker is said to have quit his job rather than work in College Hall after dark. While refusing to give details of his experiences there, the worker in question later told a reporter, "Things were just too queer there after dark. You can only explain things away for so long."

Others, too, have reported sightings of a ghostly female in College Hall. In 1991, student Robin Hinshaw told the campus newspaper, the *Collegian,* that one late autumn night, standing in the outside courtyard of the building she caught a glimpse of a face in the third floor window looking down. "It was like a white silhouette of a person . . . I got real cold real suddenly."

Morgan Streeter, a junior at Simpson in 1991, said he had a similar encounter with the ghost while he was waiting for friends in the gateway to the building one evening. Interestingly, Mr. Streeter's re-action was not one of fear. "I looked up and she was staring at me. It was peaceful, like she was talking to me," he later told the campus newspaper.

Other extraordinary stories also abound. A piano set up in the small museum section on the third floor has been heard to play a single note, over and over again, while no one is in the room. When some-one approaches the doors to the room, the sound abruptly stops and the room grows silent once more.

In October 1994, a financial aid employee was working late alone in College Hall and heard an unusual noise drifting into her office from the hallway. However, when she stepped into the hallway the sound ceased. Puzzled, she returned to her office only to hear the strange sound begin again. Once again, she checked the hallway to make sure she was alone. The corridor was empty, and the strange noise once again suddenly stopped.

Returning to her office once more, the worker reflected that there was something oddly familiar about the sound she was hearing. The third time the noise floated to her ears through the still night, she recognized the sound as that of a paper towel machine in one of the rest rooms being pulled repeatedly. Perhaps more brave than wise, she once more ventured out into the hall to find it silent. Checking both bathrooms, she found that, as she both hoped and feared, she was totally alone. Or so it seemed.

During the mid 1980s, a "phone-a-thon" fund-raising campaign was being conducted from the Red and Gold Room on the third floor of College Hall. Student volunteers were calling alumni to ask for financial support of their alma mater. However, from the very first night, things seemed a bit odd in the building. All night, students no-ticed lights flickering in the room. Phone lines that had been specially installed and checked for the event constantly went dead for no ap-parent reason. Bringing in a maintenance person to recheck all the lines did not help matters. The phone connections were found to be in good working order, but the telephones themselves continued their erratic behavior.

At one point in the evening, all the phones cut off at once. A few moments later, the lights flickered slightly as they had all evening. At this, one frustrated student volunteer yelled out, "Mildred, knock it off!" Immediately, all the phones came back to life, the lights ceased their odd flickering, and no further disturbances were noted for the rest of the evening.

By now the ghost of College Hall has become a well-known fixture on campus. Stories of the ghostly goings-on in the aged building have been told and retold through generations of college students. Articles on the ghostly reputation of the building have regularly appeared in both campus and local newspapers and have even attracted state and national attention.

On a cold night in November 1979, professional "ghost hunters" Ed and Lorraine Warren came to the Simpson campus. Investigators of ghostly phenomena for nearly twenty years, the Warrens had investigated some of the most notorious haunted houses in America.

After lecturing about ghost hunting and psychic phenomena to over three hundred students and faculty, the Warrens, accompanied by about fifty students, photographers and press entered the dark recesses of College Hall. Touring the building by candlelight, the Warrens soon claimed to determine that there was something "not of flesh and blood" inside. Afterward, Mrs. Warren told reporters, "You definitely have an earthbound spirit in the building." She described "a dark-haired girl in her twenties . . . she was wearing a skirt well down below her knees . . . she died here but convinced herself she didn't. "

Interestingly, all concerned claim that prior to their visit, the Warrens were not told anything of the nature of the ghost stories attached to the building, nor of the death of the coed so many years ago.

That same night, a student photographer also might have inadvertently captured a record of whatever wanders the dark corridors of College Hall. Walking with the group that evening, the student quickly snapped off a number of pictures of the empty building. While developing one of the shots in his darkroom the next day, he was shocked to see what some have described as the reflection of a female face in one of the photos. No such face or apparition was visible at the time he took the shot.

Since that time, other amateur and professional ghost hunters have taken their turn at investigating College Hall. Although nothing has been proven conclusively, several have reported cold drafts and "pools of energy" in the building.

Today the ghostly reputation of College Hall remains intact. Ask about the spirit among the college leadership and you will receive a variety of reactions. While a few seem to reject the legend as a fantasy that tarnishes the memory of a tragic young girl, most talk of the legend with amused skepticism. However, there are also some on the Simpson campus who take the stories of College Hall and its resident spirit seriously.

In the end, perhaps the best perspective is that of a former student writer for the Simpson newspaper, who wrote:

> People will continue to hand down ghost stories as long as floors in old buildings creak, and loose, broken shutters bang in the wind. And as long as there is Halloween, some people will claim they see mysterious lights and shadows in the third floor window of Simpson's College Hall.

2
The Return of the Gipper
University of Notre Dame
South Bend, Indiana

There are more things in heaven and earth, Horatio,
than are dempt of in your philosophy.

William Shakespeare: *Hamlet*

If one were to assemble a list of Indiana's colleges and universities, a place of honor and distinction would be obligatory for the University of Notre Dame. Founded in 1830, Notre Dame has risen to become one of the premier universities in the United States. For over 150 years, the name of Notre Dame has been synonymous with excellent academics, an outstanding student body, and especially collegiate football.

If, as some have suggested, college football is a "second religion" in America, then Notre Dame would be that religion's Mecca. Though many colleges throughout the United States can claim strong gridiron credentials, no school can boast of a longer or more vaunted football history than Notre Dame. Names such as the "Four Horsemen," Hunk Anderson, and Joe Montana have made their way from Notre Dame history into the annals of American football legend.

No name, however, is more legendary than that of the great George Gipp. Known to Notre Dame and the world as "the Gipper," his story was already well known when it was forever branded into American tradition by Ronald Reagan, who played Gipp in the 1940 movie, *Knute Rockne, All American.*

Certainly the spirit of George Gipp has woven itself into the tapestry of American sports. However, if the stories handed down for generations on the Notre Dame campus are to be believed, there is more remaining of Gipp's spirit than his name and legend. According to many, his spirit walks the floorboards at Washington Hall.

Like many sports heroes, George Gipp's beginnings were inauspicious. He was born on February 18, 1895, in the Keweenaw Peninsula of northern Michigan. The seventh of eight children, Gipp's early life hardly marked him for greatness. As a child, he excelled neither on the sports field nor the classroom. In school he was a lackluster student noted more for his frequent absences than for his academic achievement.

Though tall for his age, as a child Gipp eschewed organized sports. This changed in 1910, however, when Gipp entered Calumet High School, tried out for the school basketball team, and was given the starting position as point guard. Here for the first time his athletic

Washington Hall on the University of Notre Dame campus, where legendary football player George Gipp is said to haunt the rooms inside.

Photo: University of Notre Dame Archives

prowess began to show. Through raw and undisciplined, Gipp showed great speed and agility and an uncanny, almost ruthless competitive spirit.

However, Gipp's academics were still a sore point. Though naturally bright, his study skills and commitment to education seemed nonexistent. During his final years of high school, Gipp was noted primarily as a disciplinary problem and avid prankster. His high school principal later recalled that his chief duties during Gipp's senior year, aside from school administration, were the "once a month routine expulsion of George Gipp."

Though later Notre Dame biographies of Gipp would suggest otherwise, there is no clear record that George Gipp ever actually graduated from high school. Instead, Gipp spent much of his last year of high school at the local pool halls, betting parlors, and the YMCA, where he would occasionally become involved in informal baseball games. Though he never played organized baseball, since age eleven Gipp had taken part in sandlot games around his home town of Laurium and was known for his competitive fire and agility. Ironically, it was to be baseball that finally started Gipp on his road to greatness.

On a hot afternoon in the summer of 1916, Gipp met an old acquaintance, Wilber Gray, on a street corner in Laurium. Gray was a graduate of Notre Dame who was playing semiprofessional baseball in Elkhart, Indiana, and was back in his home town for a visit. Having seen Gipp's baseball prowess in an informal game earlier that week, Gray mentioned to Gipp that he should consider trying to get a baseball scholarship at Notre Dame. Reportedly, Gipp replied, "No, I'm too old to try school again—besides, I don't have any money."

Gray was not easily discouraged, and, with the help of several of Gipp's friends, he convinced Gipp to at least try for a scholarship. Barely a week later, having contacted his alma mater and borrowed money for the train fare to South Bend, Gray accompanied Gipp to the train station and saw him board a train that would take him to Notre Dame. Though no one knew it that day, that train would also take him to greatness, national notoriety, and ultimately death. An American football legend was in the making.

In early September Gipp was accepted as an incoming freshman at the University of Notre Dame. His first few weeks on campus were uncomfortable ones. He was older than most of the other freshman, and he was utterly destitute of funds. While he maintained passing grades in his classes, he seemed aloof and disinterested to professors and fellow classmates alike. Indeed, Gipp seemed ready to leave Notre Dame several times before fate took a hand in the autumn of 1916.

One sunny fall afternoon, Gipp went with another freshman to the football practice field to while away some free time. As they lazily kicked a football back and forth, they didn't realize they were being watched intently from the sidelines by a stocky, middle-aged man smoking a cigar. The man was Knute Rockne, fabled football coach for the Fighting Irish. Rockne was struck by the grace and natural ability of the tall boy who, seemingly without effort, routinely kicked the ball fifty yards.

Rockne approached Gipp as the young men walked off the field. Years later, Rockne would recall their first meeting:

> "What's your name?" I asked.
> Indifferently, the boy replied "Gipp, George Gipp. I come from Laurium, Michigan."
> "Played high school football?" I asked.
> "No" he said, "don't particularly care for football. Baseball's my game."
> "Put on a football suit tomorrow," I invited, "and come out with the football scrubs. I think you'll make a football player."

From such humble meetings history was made. Gipp appeared the next day on the practice field and soon won a spot on the starting lineup for Notre Dame. From the beginning he was recognized as a football phenomenon, and in his four years at Notre Dame, Gipp went on to redefine what a football player could be and propelled college football squarely into the national spotlight.

During his tenure on the Notre Dame gridiron, Gipp helped lead his team to twenty consecutive football victories and two Western Championships. Playing both offense and defense, Gipp excelled at every aspect of the game. In his career he ran the ball for 2,341 yards and passed for 1,769 yards. He ran for twenty-one touchdowns and threw another seven touchdown passes. On defense he accounted for seven interceptions and was known as a vicious tackler.

However, the end for Gipp was not far away. It is said the star that shines the brightest often fades the most quickly. The end came suddenly. In November 1920, after a game against Indiana University, Gipp began to show signs of a slight cold. Confined to bed for most of the next week, Gipp rose the next Friday to lead his team in a winning effort against Northwestern University. Though his performance in the game was, as usual, exemplary, it was clear to one and all that the Gipp was not well. On Tuesday morning, November 23, he was admitted to St. Joseph's Hospital, suffering from pneumonia.

For the next several days, as Gipp's condition worsened, Notre Dame and the entire nation held its breath. Daily reports on his condition were printed in newspapers from Los Angeles to New York. A bevy of newspaper and radio reporters camped in the lobby of St. Joseph's Hospital, waiting for word on the ailing star.

Despite consultation with leading specialists and the best care the hospital and doctors could offer, Gipp's condition continued to deteriorate. On Sunday, December 12, doctors summoned Gipp's family and Coach Rockne to his bedside. Pale and weak, Gipp motioned Rockne to listen and spoke the words that would forever seal his fate as an American legend:

> I've got to go Rock. It's all right. I'm not afraid. Some time, Rock, when the team's up against it, when things are wrong and the breaks are beating the boys—tell them to go in there with all they've got and win one for the Gipper. I don't know where I'll be then, Rock, but I'll know about it and I'll be happy.

It was poignant moment, later immortalized by Reagan on film. On Tuesday morning Gipp slipped into a coma and, early in the morning of December 15, 1920, the "immortal" George Gipp died.

On December 17, the entire student body of Notre Dame and most of the residents of South Bend turned out to see Gipp's casket as it was loaded onto a train that would ultimately take the football legend to his final resting place in Calumet, Michigan.

Commenting on the students' final farewell, one reporter commented, "As though by unspoken command a hat came off here and there, and in a flash the crowd was bareheaded. Silently, with almost defiant faces, the students gazed at the departing form of their idol. Thus ends the career of George Gipp at Notre Dame."

Owing to the gravity of the situation, the reporter's comments were logical and understandable. Subsequent events, however, might well cast a shadow of doubt on his conclusion. In fact, if one were to listen to the tales whispered throughout the years in the vicinity of Washington Hall on the Notre Dame campus, one might begin to question if something of Gipp was left behind at his beloved Notre Dame.

Washington Hall sits squarely in the center of the Notre Dame campus. It is a small, dark, Neo-Gothic building that has served for many years as the college's performing arts center, housing, in turn, the band, the orchestra, and for the last several decades, the university theater. With its high, pointed roof without and dark staircases within, the hall lends its ambiance to things dramatic, theatrical, and even mysterious.

In the early years of this century, Washington Hall was home to several student apartments. After fire destroyed much of the campus in the late 1800s, the decision was made to place student rooms in all of the major campus buildings. In addition to easing overcrowding in the dormitories, the students in each hall would serve as human alarms in case of fire or theft, since fire and security alarms were not in use at the time. Students lived in several small apartments on the upper level of the building, supervised by a "proper," or dormitory supervisor, who lived on the first floor. It was up to this individual, usually a brother from the Order of the Holy Cross, to watch over the building, and to impose university discipline on those under his care.

In its time Washington Hall has been home to a great many students, including a future dean of the Notre Dame Law School and several future leaders of business. While university housing records from the time are unclear, legend has it that Washington was also home to George Gipp during his last semester at Notre Dame. Further, the tale holds that Washington Hall contributed to Gipp's untimely demise.

According to the old story, Gipp, who was notorious for flouting university rules, had been caught coming in past student curfew several times that semester. The proper, a stern monk named Brother Maurilius, had repeatedly warned Gipp and finally had threatened that the next time he came in late, he would face disciplinary proceedings that would eliminate him from the sports program. Uncharacteristically, Gipp seemed to have taken the threat seriously.

For a short period he was careful to make his appearance before the 11:00 P.M. curfew. However, in mid-November Gipp found himself ambling back to campus from a night in town later than the university deemed proper. As he silently made his way across campus toward Washington Hall, a nearby clock on campus struck out the midnight hour, and Gipp remembered the venerable brother's threat. Rather than risking the ire of Brother Maurilius, Gipp rashly decided to sleep outside on the steps of Washington Hall instead. Though mild for November, the night was chill and damp, and, according to legend, when Gipp awoke the next morning, he felt the first chills and sore throat that would later grow into pneumonia and, ultimately, take his life.

The story of Gipp sleeping on the steps of Washington Hall is, of course, the stuff of legend. Little can be learned about the veracity of such a tale. More clear, however, are the mysterious events that began in Washington Hall immediately after Gipp's death—events that were linked in the minds of all those involved with the fated star and his death.

The events in question started just after the students' return from Christmas break in the first days of 1921. The first to notice something strange going on in the building was band student Jim Clancy. Clancy, who played first trumpet in the school orchestra, was alone in the band room on the first floor one evening practicing a difficult trumpet piece for an upcoming concert.

As he later related the experience, he was taking a break from his practicing when he heard a strange sound coming from the other end of the room. Investigating, Clancy quickly discovered that the sound, which he described as a kind of "low moan," was in fact emanating from a tuba stacked along the far wall. Then, as suddenly as it began, the sound abruptly ended. Thinking it odd, Clancy quickly picked up his music and turned to leave, only to have the sound come once again from the instrument. As he later declared, "That horn was playing itself!"

Fearing the ridicule of other band students if he told his story, Clancy decide to keep the event to himself. Within a few days, however, others began to hear the sound as well. Joe Shanahan, a student living in the hall, was the first resident to hear the sound several nights later, as he was attempting to sneak into the dormitory after hours. As he passed the band room on his way up the stairs toward his room, a low moan came out of the dark air and seemed to fill the building around him. Later, Shanahan would recount that, as he turned and started toward the source of the sound, he saw a sort of "gossamer haze" floating over the band room. Wasting no time in his escape, Shanahan bolted upstairs to his room to find the other residents of the hall asleep, seemingly oblivious to the sound that had so upset him.

If most of the residents of Washington Hall were still unaware of the phenomena occurring around them, they would soon no longer have that luxury. Several nights later, another student, Harry Stevenson, who lived in a nearby residence hall, was visiting friends who lived in Washington Hall. As the dreaded 11:00 P.M. curfew drew near, Stevensen bid farewell to his friends and began to climb the steps down toward the main entrance of the hall . As he came abreast of the first floor landing, he too heard the sound of a musical instrument, this time a bugle, float through the darkened hall. Suddenly the note ceased, to be replaced by what he later described as a "weird howling moan." So startling were the sounds that Stevensen collapsed in hysterics on the steps, to be found several minutes later by his friends, who had heard the sound and his cries. Immediately the lamps were lit and the band room searched, but apparently it was empty.

Strange as these occurrences were, they were only the beginning. Whoever or whatever was afoot in Washington Hall was just getting warmed up. Soon the eerie sounds in the dead of night became a regular occurrence for the young men living there. Moreover, they were now accompanied by the sound of footsteps as well.

One resident at the time described hearing the sound of an instrument at midnight, followed by running steps coming directly up the staircase toward the student living quarters. Immediately he and several other students ran to the landing, thinking they might finally catch the prankster who had been disturbing their sleep for weeks. Together they gathered on the third floor landing and, though they could clearly hear the steps approaching them, they could see nothing on the stairs.

Now the phenomena began to widen in scope. Doors slammed when there was no one in the vicinity. One student, leaving his living quarters, felt a hand push him while walking down the steps past the band room. Objects began to disappear from the residents' rooms, only to have them turn up in odd places.

These strange phenomena attracted the attention of the student body. Soon it seemed everyone on campus was claiming an encounter with the famed ghost of Washington Hall. One student even claimed that, as he was passing Washington Hall one night, he saw a ghostly figure on horseback ride through campus and up the steps of the building, only to disappear on the doorstep. The figure on the horse, he swore, was none other than George Gipp.

Soon the faculty became aware of the stories. A group of students, led by professor "Doc" Conell, decide to spend the night in the band room in order to disprove the wild tales spreading through campus. By their own accounts, they were rewarded in their venture by the customary unearthly sounds in the room, a filmy substance appearing in one corner, and by having one student pushed from his cot by unseen hands.

A carnival atmosphere soon began to pervade Washington Hall as more and more curious students tried their hand at "laying" the ghost. In the midst of this, however, only one person remained unaffected and unconvinced. The staid Brother Maurilius remained unabashedly skeptical about the unearthly events. He claimed to have never heard nor seen anything out of the ordinary and seemed willing to write the entire episode off as student pranks and mass hysteria.

Such was his attitude until one night when he was awakened from his sleep by a sound he later described as "a cross between a crash and an explosion" coming from the stairway. Thinking something heavy might somehow have been dropped there, he ran to the stairway, only to see nothing out of place. Then, suddenly, he too heard the mournful notes emanating from the band room. Convinced now that he was the victim of a hoax, Brother Maurilius ran to the band room and searched it, but found it empty. Next he went to the rooms of the student residents, only to find them asleep. Rudely awakening his young charges, Brother Maurilius demanded an explanation, but none was offered. "Brother," said one student, "now you get what we have been living with for these past weeks. Are you convinced yet?"

Convinced he was. The next morning Brother Maurilius appeared in the office of Father Charles O'Donnell, provincial head of the Order of the Holy Cross, and demanded something be done. Later that day, Brother Maurilius was seen leading O'Donnell on a tour of the building. Though seemingly skeptical, the priest promised the Brother "a full investigation."

What was done, if anything, at the good Brother's behest is unknown. The stories of the ghost of Washington Hall seemed to have quieted some in succeeding years, only to be revived again in 1945 when residents reported hearing footsteps on the roof of the building in the dead of night and seeing lights that mysteriously turned themselves off and on.

The years have brought their changes to Washington Hall. The band room has since been converted into classrooms and an experimental theater. Since the 1950s Washington Hall has ceased housing students on a regular basis, but some people have continued to experience unsettling phenomena there. One student, working late one evening setting lights for an upcoming production, was startled to see a light bulb he had just screwed in unscrew itself before his eyes and crash to the floor beneath his ladder.

Phil McElroy, a student who lived in the hall one summer, told the campus newspaper, "There were too many things that I could not account for—lights would go on by themselves and doors would slam." McElroy then went on to relate the story of a youth he knew who felt a hand on his shoulder while climbing the main stairs. He turned quickly to find himself alone. Other students who have stayed in the hall also have heard the slamming of doors and the sound of phantom footsteps on the stairs.

In 1968, four Notre Dame juniors decided to spend the night in the hall to investigate the story. The group sneaked into the hall at 11:00 P.M. one Sunday evening, carrying with them an armload of photographic equipment and audiotape devices to record anything that might happen. As one student set up his camera on stage to pose for some spurious "spirit" pictures, another student went to the back of the theater to playfully turn off the lights. After he had done so, however, he found that he could not turn them on again. "The light switch refused to stay in the on position," he later reported to the school newspaper.

Left in compete darkness, the group was suddenly paralyzed by the sound of footsteps in the hallway and a glowing light that appeared in the center of the seating area, accompanied by a moan that reverberated through the entire chamber. Now truly shaken, the group ran for the exit, never to return.

Not all encounters with the Washington Hall spirit have been so intimidating. For some students, the ghost has seemed benign and even helpful. In the mid 1980s, student Lorri Wright was in a play produced at Washington Hall. One night she and several cast members decided to stay late and contact the apparition if possible. After play practice was over, one student hid in the catwalks while the director secured the building for the night and left. The cast member then climbed down and let Lorri and several others in through a side entrance where they were waiting in the shadows. The students climbed back onto the stage and lit candles. One student produced a Ouija board brought along for the occasion, and two of the participants placed their fingers on it.

"We asked it if there was anyone in the hall that wanted to speak to us," Lorri now recalls, "and the plactett immediately slid to the letters "S-G," and then slid over to the part of the board that reads "good-bye." Questioning what such a missive might mean, the students retried the experiment, only to receive the message "S-G—good-bye" again. Now suddenly unsure of themselves, the students decided to abort their seance, and, packing up their belongings, silently exited by the side entrance.

"As soon as we were out," Lorri says, "we looked back and saw a weird light shining through the window by the theater. Then it was gone, and in a second it appeared again in the stairwell, coming toward the door we had just left. We all dove in the bushes just as the door opened—and a Notre Dame Security Guard stepped out. S-G—Security Guard. I think whatever was there was trying to keep us from getting in trouble. From then on, we always had the feeling the ghost was on our side."

Today Washington Hall sits quietly amid the splendor of the Notre

Dame campus. Hall director Tom Barkes says that, while he occasionally hears odd sounds, he believes them to be just the customary sounds of an old building. "If there is a ghost at Washington Hall, I have yet to meet him—George Gipp or no!" declares Barkes.

Yet the stories continue. Through the years other possible explanations for the haunting have been forwarded. Some have suggested the ghost is that of a steeplejack killed in the construction of the building. Others tell of a student killed while working on a play. However, sooner or later most of these stories come back to George Gipp, the legendary Gipper.

No one can doubt that Gipp's spectacular career and untimely death left an indelible mark on the University of Notre Dame. The persona of the Gipper will forever symbolize what Notre Dame football is all about. Still, one could well question if that is the only legacy Gipp left to the university he loved. Some might argue that he also left a part of himself—a wondering, roguish spirit that will forever wander the floors of Washington Hall.

3

The Phantom of the Purple Masque, "Duncan," and Other Ghosts of Kansas State
Kansas State University
Manhattan, Kansas

Life's but a walking shadow, a poor player,
that struts and frets his hour upon the stage and then is heard no more.
William Shakespeare: *Macbeth*

When one thinks of Kansas, one pictures the Great Plains, quaint farmhouses, and an endless sea of wheat fields stretching as far as the eye can see. A drive through the central part of the state confirms the impression of the wholesome, prosaic Midwest. However, in the town of Manhattan there stands an institution that seems to contrast sharply with the agrarian simplicity of Kansas—at least, if one believes its ghost stories.

Kansas State University lies on 668 acres near downtown Manhattan. While located squarely in the center of the Great Plains, the university itself is hardly the stereotypical Midwestern college. In its architecture and ambiance, Kansas State resembles one of the older Ivy League colleges that dot the east coast of the U.S. This striking impression is no accident. Founded in 1863, Kansas State University from its very inception was designed to have the look and feel of an older eastern university, according to university officials.

If that was the plan, then it proved most successful. Strolling through the campus at dusk on a spring evening, past the flowering shrubs and trees that dot the landscape, one might easily imagine that the entire college has been uprooted from its natural place along the Atlantic coast and transplanted, whole, to the Midwestern farmland.

Perhaps it is this very Gothic atmosphere that has, over the years, produced not one but a legion of ghostly tales surrounding Kansas

State. Some might scoff at these stories, but no one can dispute that, despite its practical, no-nonsense setting, Kansas State may well be one of the most haunted universities in America.

The Phantom of the Purple Masque

Many colleges across the nation can boast of a resident "theater ghost," but none seems to do so with more pride that Kansas State University. Bearing the evocative title of the "Purple Masque," the theater in question is attached to East Stadium on the Kansas State campus.

Construction on the building was first begun in 1922 as an athletic center and dormitory. Monies for the structure were donated by students, faculty and alumni in honor of Kansas State students who had given their lives for their country in World War I. The east and west wings, as well as the attached intramural field, were completed by 1924. The facility was a center for intercollegiate and intramural sports and served as a dormitory for those involved in the school athletic teams.

Photo: Kansas State University Archives

The entrance to the Purple Masque Theater, where a phantom is said to make its home.

Time and university development have wrought their changes on the facility. In 1964 the athletic dormitory was moved to another building on campus and the cafeteria was converted into the Purple Masque. In 1964 a new stadium was completed to host university football games, and in 1985, most of the college's theater productions were moved to the new Nichols Theater. Presently, the aging facility is used mainly for painting and sculpting classes and as the administrative center for the University Police Department. However, in the midst of all the changes, the Purple Masque remains. In the most recent decades, the small auditorium has been used as an experimental theater and as home to student-produced plays.

The building itself seems a suitable setting for a ghost story. Outside, an ivy-covered arch frames the building, replete with an ornate wrought iron gate. Inside, the Purple Masque is a dim chamber with black walls, a plywood stage, a tiny sound and light booth, seating for about one hundred, and nothing more.

Yet, if the many stories of the place are to be believed, there may well be something else residing within the walls of the Purple Masque—an eerie presence that walks the floors at night. This presence has given rise to innumerable tales that confound logic and stretch the imagination. He is known to all associated with the theater as "Nick." Like many ghosts, his background is the subject of debate and speculation.

Long-held university legend states that Nick was a student athlete at Kansas State during the middle part of this century. According to the old tale, Nick was a football player who was hit in the solar plexus one day during a practice game. Hurt but not in apparent danger, Nick was taken from the football field by the team trainer and laid on a table in the cafeteria, where he could rest and recover. Since his injury did not appear to be severe, the trainer then returned to his duties on the practice field. However, when the coach and trainer returned to the cafeteria a few minutes later to check on their charge, they found him dead. His injuries had evidently been far more serious than they appeared.

It should be noted that official university records show no record of such an event. Officials point out that while one young man did die during an intramural football game during the 1950s, he was not in East Stadium at the time of his death.

However, official records matter little where legends are concerned, and since the dormitory cafeteria was renovated into the Purple Masque, the story of the doomed football player was handed down from generation to generation until it became accepted as fact among the students. Moreover, the story of this ill-fated athlete has been used to explain the many mysterious events which have taken place at the Purple Masque.

The first person to encounter the strange presence in the theater was Carl Hinrichs, who came to the university in 1964 as an assistant speech professor. Although Hinrichs has publicly professed himself to be a skeptic on all matters ghostly, he is at a loss to explain the strange event that occurred one night at the Purple Masque, soon after he arrived at Kansas State.

Preparing for a production of *My Fair Lady*, Hinrichs was in the theater alone late one night painting a background flat to be used in the performance. In preparation for his task, Hinrichs walked to a backstage room to mix a five-gallon bucket of paint. Once the paint was readied, he left the bucket standing in the middle of the floor and walked back to the stage area, moving the flat to a position where it could be readily accessible.

While on stage, the professor was startled to hear a loud crash from the storeroom he had just left. He called out, "Who's there?" and ran back to the storeroom to find the bucket turned upside down in the middle of the room, a thin sea of paint spreading from it to cover the floor. As Hinrichs would later tell the campus newspaper, the *Collegian,* "I looked around for an animal . . . anything, but no one was around. Then I hosed the paint down the floor drain and got out. The Masque was completely locked, and no one else could have gotten in." He concluded his comment by adding, "I cannot confirm or deny any other happenings. All I know is what happened to me."

As inauspicious as this encounter might seem, it would not be the last appearance of the Phantom of the Purple Masque. Perhaps the most persistently reported phenomena are the sound of footsteps echoing through empty hallways at the Masque. At times the maintenance staff has tried to put these stories to rest by explaining them as the sound of water pipes banging in the old building. However, this does not adequately explain all of the occurrences which have surfaced in the last several years. Once, while alone in the building with a friend, Mark Grimes, former president of the K-State Players, heard footsteps pacing back and forth in an upstairs hallway. Alarmed, since the building was locked and supposedly vacant, the two went upstairs, only to find the hallway in silence. Undaunted, the intrepid pair turned on the lights, illuminating the area brightly, stationed themselves on either end of the hallway, and waited for the footsteps to return.

They did. In a few moments, the sound of footsteps was clearly heard echoing up and down the corridor between them. In the close confines of the hallway, Grimes and his friend could follow the progress of the footsteps, an unseen pressure making a number of the floorboards creak, but there was no visible source for the sounds.

Hal Knowles, shop foreman in 1969, confirmed in the *Collegian* that he too has heard the spectral footsteps. "He does most of his walking from midnight on," Knowles reported. "Upstairs you can hear a door creaking before he begins his walk. One night I heard him coming down the hall again. I quietly stepped to the doorway and waited. When I could hear him right outside the door, I threw the door open. The footsteps stopped but there was no one there."

Knowles also reported other experiences with Nick. "Another time I was crawling through the tunnel where we store the props. I had the weird sensation that somebody was in the tunnel besides me. When I turned to pick up a flat, something touched me on the shoulder. It felt like a hand. I turned around and there was no one there."

Nick has made himself heard and felt to many habituates of the Masque in the last three decades. Dennis Good, who graduated in 1987, also had a late-night experience with Nick. He reported that one night he was alone in the theater practicing a dance routine for an upcoming production. When his dance brought him a little too close to the edge of the stage, he lost his footing and began to topple headlong toward the floor below. He later said that as he pitched forward, he felt a pair of hands gently catch him and lift him back on to the stage.

"I saw him last year during rehearsals for a play," K-State senior Jennifer Collins told the campus newspaper in 1995. Collins went on to relate that she and two other students entered the building to go to rehearsal, walked up the main stairway, and saw a silhouette that moved in front of them and went through a closed door. "Then the door started moving like someone had walked through the door and it was swinging back and forth," Collins reported. "We all stood there in shock, and then I said, 'The door is moving, the door is moving!' " Summoning all of his courage, one of her companions opened the door and looked in but quickly shut it again. Collins told the campus newspaper her friend claimed that he had seen a white vaporous form in the room but "did not stick around to find out what it was." Adopting the better part of valor, they quickly ran from the hallway.

This was not be Collins's only confrontation with the ghost. She also reported that, a few months later, she and another student were in the dressing room readying themselves for a rehearsal when they heard a banging noise resounding through the room. Collins reportedly remarked to her fellow student that the noise was probably "just Nick," but her friend tried to explain the sound away as simply steam pipes banging. They argued about it for a moment and then, on a whim, Collins called out, "OK, Nick, stop it!" In that instant, the pounding stopped and all was quiet for the rest of the night.

According to the legends, Nick was particularly active between 1964 and 1969. Dave Laughlin, a foreman for the theater at that time, is said to have had several encounters with Nick. The most striking of these came one evening when he was alone in the sound booth taping sound cues for an upcoming production. With the hour growing late and his task nearly finished, Laughlin decided to review the tape he had just made and then close up for the evening. He was a bit unnerved, to say the least, when after rewinding the tape, he replayed it and heard, overlaid against the sounds he had just finished recording, a cheery voice clearly saying, "Hi, Dave!"

Nick's pranks, while almost playful at times, have also been unnerving and sometimes frightening to the novice actors at the Masque. One night a few years ago, a young freshman actress found herself alone in a dressing room waiting to go on stage. The small dressing room held a desk on which sat several decorative wooden cubes stacked one on top of another. As the young actress was between scenes, she shut the door, made a quick costume change, and sat down at the desk to rest until her stage cue. She was bewildered to see one of the wooden cubes on the desk before her rising up into the air, turning slowly, and then floating down, landing at her feet. While badly frightened, the girl quickly remembered the stories of the ghost she had heard and managed to mutter, "Not nice, Nick!" as she hurriedly rose to leave the room.

When she got to the door, she risked a glance over her shoulder at the desk she had just vacated. Strangely, the cube was no longer on the floor where it had so unceremoniously floated a moment before. Instead, it was back to its original position atop the other cubes on the desk. As the alarmed actress later told her director, "It was absolutely not an hallucination—it happened in front of my eyes and I know what I saw!"

Nick's other activities have been even more direct and, at times, shocking. Another inexplicable Purple Masque incident involved two technicians who were working late one night in the theater. At about 2:00 A.M. they decided to take a brief rest before completing their task of setting up lighting for an upcoming play. Since the set on which they were working included a bed and couch, they decide to use these props for an impromptu catnap and lay down.

They had not slept long before the young man on the couch struggled awake, coughing and gasping for breath. Squinting through one eye, he saw a fire extinguisher discharging toward him from mid-air. This alone was enough to startle the young stagehand, but what chilled his blood was the fact that no one was holding the device. It seemed, he later reported, to be hanging in thin air. As the nozzle of the device zeroed in on him, spraying the malevolent chemical into his face, both students ran from the building, locking it behind them. Understandably, they refused to enter again until the morning light.

Not all of Nick's escapades have been quite so malicious. At times, Nick has been known to be quite helpful. Such was the experience related by Kay Coles, a former theater major at K-State. Coles told a reporter that a crew once unloaded chairs in the Masque to be set up later for a performance that night. The men piled the chairs backstage and went outside to unload more equipment. Hearing a commotion in the theater, the men walked back into the empty auditorium to see all the chairs neatly set up and programs set in place on the seats. "There was no one around," Coles told the reporter. "It all happened in less than five minutes, where normally it takes a crew of five people at least half an hour to do that job."

While Nick has made his presence known many times over the succeeding years, it has fallen to only a few people to actually catch a glimpse of him. One of them was Charlotte Mcfarland, an assistant professor of speech. Working late with two of her acting students, Mcfarland glanced back and noticed someone standing at the back-stage entrance. Thinking it was a student, the professor approached the figure and politely asked, "Can I help you?" When the figure did not respond, she became more direct, asking, "Excuse me, but are you supposed to be here?" At that point, one of the acting students saw the strange figure and screamed.

Startled, Mcfarland jumped and looked toward the student, but a split second later, when she looked back toward the figure, it had vanished. Now totally perplexed, she went through the door to the backstage area but found it empty. Mcfarland later told a reporter, "I suppose it could have been someone hiding backstage but I don't think it was. Now that I look back upon it, chasing whoever or whatever I chased was probably a stupid idea."

Others, too, have reported glimpsing an enigmatic figure within the precincts of the Purple Masque. Professor Mcfarland also relates the story of four students in her Fundamentals of Acting class who looked up to see an "iridescent face" looking down at them from the locked lighting booth as they were practicing on stage one night. "As they stood and talked about it, it slowly disappeared," Mcfarland re-counts. When the students later unlocked the booth to turn out the stage lights, the lights would not go off. One of the students called out "Nick, please let us out. Let us go home." The lights went out—all of them, even the exit lights above the doors. The students had to grope their way out of the darkened theater. "This is really typical,"

Mcfarland concludes. "Almost everyone who has worked in the Masque has experienced something."

Student Patti Writz told the *Collegian* that she also believes she might have seen Nick:

> We were getting notes for the play *From Heaven to Hell* when I looked back and saw someone staring at us through the slats at the back of the stage. Another cast member, Mark Pennington, got up to see who it was. He looked behind the door and saw a man standing there just watching. He could not get a good view of him, however. Mark came back and told us what he had seen so we all went back there and when we did, he was gone. But there had been no footsteps or the sound of a door closing. It was like he had just disappeared.

Through the years, an amazing number of students and staff are said to have encountered the Phantom of the Purple Masque. While some still scoff at the stories, others sincerely believe that something mysterious stalks the boards of the small stage. Whether it is the doomed spirit of a college athlete who met an untimely death or some other wayward specter will never be truly known.

Duncan and Other Ghosts of the Greek System

While the Phantom of the Purple Masque may well be the most celebrated spirit at Kansas State, he is not the only ghostly presence associated with the campus. If the stories told by many local fraternities are true, then Nick has a host of otherworldly confederates at Kansas State. No fewer than five fraternities at Kansas State count spectral residents among their rolls.

Kappa Sigma fraternity has long been the site of tales of a ghostly occupant named Irving. According to legend, Irving is the spirit of a former member who hung himself in the file room of the fraternity many years ago. This spirit manifests himself as a "white haze" that has been seen throughout the house. Fraternity member Mike Dahl recently told a local newspaper, "Several years ago, four or five guys were playing cards in the housemother's room, which is close to the stairs and the front door. They heard a noise upstairs and since it was vacation and no one was supposed to be in the house, they ran upstairs to see who is was. When they got to the top of the stairs, one member saw a white haze, like a ghost."

Another member tells the story of working in the house one summer break when he and a roommate happened to be the only people in the residence. At about 2:00 A.M. he was painting a hallway when, out of the corner of his eye, he glimpsed a figure moving past him. He turned and saw the figure of a man who promptly vanished before his eyes. He and his roommate searched the house, but it was empty.

Another report tells of a student who was staying in the house alone during a break. Studying in his room, the young man turned his radio up to maximum, but his reverie was disturbed by someone asking him to "turn it down." Out of reflex, the young man called out "OK" and reached out for the volume control. Before his hand reached the knob, the student remembered he was alone in the house.

Delta Sigma Phi is another fraternity that plays a role in the ghostlore of the campus community. The house that is now home to the fraternity was built as a YMCA many years ago and was then converted into St. Mary's Hospital for a time before housing the fraternity. At the conclusion of the building's tenure as a hospital, an event occurred that would give rise to its ghostly reputation.

On the day the hospital was moving to its new location, hospital attendants arrived to transport the patients by ambulance to the new facility. According to the old tale, when the transfer was completed, one patient was missing. An elderly man named George Segal had rolled from his bed and had become wedged between it and the wall. When the orderlies came to check the room, Segal could not be seen, and, assuming he had already been transported to the new hospital, they moved on to other rooms on the floor. Their oversight was not discovered until the next day. By that time it was too late, as Segal had asphyxiated during the night. His body was removed, but legends suggest his spirit has never left the place of his passing.

Through the years that Delta Sigma Phi has occupied the residence, "George" has made his presence known in a number of ways. Lights are said to often turn themselves off and on of their own volition. Objects move by themselves, and odd sounds have been heard late at night, most emanating from the third floor room where George Segal died.

Daryl Reinke is a former member who claims to have encountered the spirit. In 1993, Reinke told the *Collegian* that one night when he was a pledge, he and his roommates heard a sound coming from the middle of their bedroom as they were trying to fall asleep. At first they thought it might be coming from a neighboring room, or perhaps it was the building's air conditioning system. However, as the noise continued, they realized it was a voice coming from thin air in the middle of their room. "It kinda made a believer out of me when it happened," Reinke remarked in the article. "It was definitely unexplainable."

According to the same article, one night in 1992, student Jerrod Overly was in his room on the third floor of the fraternity when he noticed his doorknob rattling. Curious, he turned off the TV and went to the door. However, as he approached, the rattling stopped. A split second later he threw the door open but found the long corridor empty. Overly's room is directly across the hall from the room where George is said to have met his fate.

Maybe the strangest aspect of the legend of Delta Sigma Phi is the story that George apparently has an affinity for the television series "Star Trek." In 1973, an ice storm caused the power at the Delta Phi house, as well as the surrounding area, to be off for several days. However, members claim that the power at the fraternity would came back on every afternoon just in time to watch Star Trek and then go off again afterward. A check of the surrounding houses revealed that the power had come on only for the Delta Phi house. Perhaps George simply wanted his entertainment.

If the spirit of the long-dead patient George Segal does indeed inhabit the Delta Sigma Phi house, he might have company. It is said that the ghostly form of a nurse has also been seen in the house on several occasions. Witnesses say she carries a candle and tray of medicine and has been known to walk through the main room of the fraternity, only disappear from sight. If the stories are true, one might wonder if the nurse is searching for her lost patient, George Segal, who was left behind so many years ago.

Other fraternities also claim ghostly presences. The Triangle fraternity is said to be haunted by a spectral woman and two young children. She is said to be the wife of a doctor who once lived there.

Children's voices have been heard giggling late at night, and at least one member of the fraternity is said to have been disturbed by the sounds of footsteps in the downstairs kitchen. Searching the building to make sure he was alone, the young man entered the fraternity office and saw the hazy figure of a woman staring at him. He promptly fled to the safety of his room and locked himself in for the night. Like a proper lady, the spirit declined to follow.

The home of Lambda Chi Alpha on Denison Avenue is said to be haunted by the ghost known as "Polli Pi Phi," after a sorority that occupied the building before Lambda Chi took possession. According to the tale, the unfortunate young woman was bathing one night in an upstairs bathroom when a hair dryer, still plugged in, fell into the bathtub and electrocuted her. This event forms the basis of stories of a young woman seen walking down the hallways late at night. Unlike other late night female guests sometimes found in the fraternity, this young girl is seen to enter the upstairs bathroom and never emerge. In this same bathroom, lights have been known to turn off and on for no apparent reason.

Of all the ghost stories associated with the Greek system at Kansas State, the most notable is a spirit named "Duncan," who is said to haunt the Pi Kappa Phi fraternity on Fairchild Street.

The building that Pi Kappa Phi now occupies has a long history of association with the Greek system. Its first occupants were the members of the Theta Chi Fraternity. After their departure, the house changed hands several times, with different fraternities owning the building, until 1993 when Phi Kappa Phi took possession. The origins of the ghostly legend of the structure are traced back to its first occupants, Theta Chi. According to the story, Duncan was a Theta Chi pledge who died during an fraternity initiation ceremony.

Stories very slightly on the cause of his demise. One legend states that Duncan was going through a ritual "paddling" common years ago on college campuses. Supposedly, when first struck with the paddle, Duncan, still in a crouched position, turned to avoid another blow and received the second impact on the head. The impact fractured his skull and killed him. An even stranger version of this legend suggest that Duncan suffered a fatal heart attack after being forced into a coffin during an initiation ceremony. A third variant says that Duncan fell or was pushed down a flight of stairs during the final "Hell Week" of pledging.

Whatever the cause of Duncan's demise, his spirit has long been said to reside in the building. The spirit is said to manifest itself in some creative and unsettling ways. The most infamous of these manifestations centers around a pledge paddle left hanging on the library wall when the Fiji Fraternity moved into the house after it was vacated by Theta Chi.

Rick Lawrence, a former member of the Fiji Fraternity, which purchased the house from Theta Chi, recalled to a reporter:

> When we bought the house two paddles were still hanging on the wall of what is now the library. One of them had Duncan's name on it. We threw the paddles away but when we started painting the wall, the image of Duncan's paddle kept reappearing. We painted over it three or four times but it kept on coming back. The other paddle never reappeared, but outline of the paddle with the name "Duncan" on it kept coming back. Finally we just paneled over it.

When the fraternity building was eventually sold to the Pi Kappa Phi's, the paneling in the library was removed. The new owners were amazed to find that the image of the paddle had reappeared once again. The wall was covered with spackle and then painted a deep red, but the outline of the paddle persisted. Finally, out of desperation, the fraternity wallpapered the upper section of the wall and placed paneling on the lower section to cover the telltale mark.

Although this memorial of the ill-fated Duncan has been covered over, other reminders have remained. Through the years, members of each group that has occupied the residence have described inexplicable events which have occurred there. Perhaps one of the most evocative of these eerie happenings was described in the *Collegian* several years ago by student writer Carol Holstead:

> It was early October. All was still in the K-State Phi Gamma Delta fraternity house. Don Clancy, intent on his studying, stopped momentarily to glance at the clock. 1:30 AM. Suddenly Don shivered. The temperature in his room had dropped noticeably. Don heard a crunching sound. Someone shuffled through the leaves as they walked down the outside stairway. In the fall, the huge elm tree in the backyard

dumped its leaves into the stairwell, making it easy to hear people as they walked. Don opened the door to his room and looked out into the hall. No one was there, but the sound of crunching leaves persisted. Don went outside to look and took a close look at the stairs. No, it couldn't be, but it was. Someone, or something was coming down those stairs. And it was leaving the definite impression of footprints in the leaves on every step as it approached. Don ran back to his room and slammed the door. "It couldn't be a ghost" he thought. "I am only a pledge, and it's probably someone playing a trick on me." Don crept back to his door and eased it open just enough to take a peek into the hall. He was convinced. The ghost was checking each door along the hall by turning the doorknob. Then it was gone.

Rod Smith, an alumnus of Phi Gamma Delta, also reported hearing a noise outside his door one night a few years ago. When he looked out, Smith saw what he later described as a "ghastly face" staring at him. He quickly shut his door and never again saw the face.

Larry Keller, another fraternity member, told the *Collegian* in 1995, "I am not a big fan of the ghost." He told the newspaper that he was in the fraternity bathroom one night brushing his teeth when the bathroom door suddenly shut. Then the bathroom fan turned on and went off again. When this occurred a second time, Keller checked the fuse to see if it was bad. It was not, and he found that fan had been in the off position the entire time. "Needless to say, I took off as fast as I could. I finished brushing my teeth in the kitchen," Keller said.

Also according to the *Collegian,* former student Andy McHart had another strange encounter while living in the house. "I was going upstairs to get my alarm clock in the sleeping dorms" said McHart. "When I was halfway up the stairs, the railing started rattling and shaking all on its own. Then I heard footsteps coming up behind me like someone pounding up the stairs really fast. They passed right by me and I did not see anyone on the stairs. I didn't get my alarm clock, and I didn't sleep up there anymore. It was a eerie feeling."

As uncanny as many of Duncan's manifestations have been, in at least one instance his interventions may have averted tragedy in the Phi Gamma Delta house. On January 29, 1995, members of the fraternity sleeping in the upstairs dormitory were awakened by smoke lofting through their sleeping area. The fire was contained quickly and little damaged was done to the dormitory. Later, fire officials credited quick action on behalf of the fraternity brothers present at the time of the fire with containing it. However, according to at least one member of the fraternity, it may be Duncan the ghost who deserved the credit.

Shaun Pickering, a freshman member, told the campus newspaper that early that morning, he had been awakened in his bed by a movement in the room. Struggling groggily awake, Pickering saw the figure of someone walk past him toward the east wall of the sleeping dorm. The figure carefully shut and locked the south window of the sleeping room, then exited via the east side. While it was not uncommon for a member to open or shut the windows of the sleeping dormitory at night, there were several aspects to this figure that disturbed the young man. One was the fact that, though he could see it clearly in the early morning light, the figure did not appear to resemble any of the current active members of the house. The second puzzle in this strange tableau was the fact that, though the figure walked the length of the sleeping dormitory, he made absolutely no sound as he walked.

Further, a group of men outside the east door later stated that they did not see or hear anyone come from the room that morning. As Pickering told a reporter, "You can hear before anyone gets there. It is pretty loud. If anyone human was moving around, they should have heard him in the next room or seen him go out."

What makes this bizarre incident even more significant is that, scarcely half an hour later, an old electric blanket in the dormitory began to smolder and smoke. Attempting to clear the room of smoke, several men tried to open the south window, which had been open just a short time but now before refused to budge. Finally, the men opened the door to the sleeping area, but the fresh air fanned the smoldering embers in the blanket into open flame.

While the fire was quickly controlled, it has been pointed out that had the south window had been left open, the fresh air might have fanned the flames much more quickly and the results to the sleeping men might have been disastrous. According to some of the men in the room at the time, Duncan had intervened to prevent a tragedy for them and severe damage to the house he has occupied for many years.

Such are the tales that have been collected for many years at Kansas State University. It is possible that they are all the stuff of whim and hearsay. However, in researching the history of these tales, one is struck by the sheer volume and consistency of the reports. These stories are all part of the rich tapestry of tradition attached to this lovely campus, which may well be one of the most haunted in our nation.

4

The Curse of Rafinesque
Transylvania University
Lexington, Kentucky

Damn thee and thy school as I place curses upon you.

Constantine Samuel Rafinesque

Can the curse of an eccentric professor, dead some 150 years, stretch across the mists of time to affect the living with unfortunate and inexplicable results? The skeptic would scoff at such a suggestion, but on the campus of Transylvania University in Lexington, Kentucky, there are those who believe it more than just possible. And, if you have the time, they will take you to a musty, dark tomb and tell you the story of the curse of Rafinesque.

Transylvania University is a small liberal arts college situated on about six blocks of downtown Lexington. In size and appearance, it resembles many such schools across the United States. However, in the late eighteenth and early nineteenth centuries, Transylvania University was considered one of the premier academic institutions in the country and became known as the "Tutor to the West."

Chartered in 1780, Transylvania College educated scores of congressmen, governors, business leaders and diplomats, from Stephen F. Austin to Jefferson Davis. It offered one of the first medical and law schools in the western states and gained renown as an institution of high academic reputation. Such was its fame that Thomas Jefferson, complaining about his difficulties in starting a state college in Virginia, wrote to a friend in 1820:

> We must send our children for education to Kentucky [Transylvania College] or to Cambridge [Harvard]. The latter will return them to us

fanatics and Tories and the former will keep them to add to their
population. If we are to go begging anywhere for an education, I would
rather it should be to Kentucky because she has more the flavor of the
old cask than any other.

Due to the excellent reputation of Transylvania University, both
students and professors flocked to its doors from across the nation
and around the world. Of all who passed through its hallowed halls,
however, none has been the subject of more conjecture and controversy than Constantine Rafinesque.

By the time Rafinesque came to Transylvania University in 1818,
his fortune and fame had already been made. He was respected as a
man of intellect and great knowledge, and was one of the premiere
naturalists in America. He was born on October 22, 1783, in the European capital of Constantinople, the son of a traveling textile merchant.
Much of his early years were spent in Marseilles, France, where, as he
later wrote, "Among the flowers and fruits I began to enjoy life and I
became a botanist." After leaving Marseilles, Rafinesque studied
throughout Europe, applying his considerable intellectual abilities to
the fields of botany, philosophy and biology. Rafinesque also became
a student of the classics and became conversant in seven languages.

In 1802, he and a brother sailed to America to take positions in a
Philadelphia counting house. He applied himself energetically to his
business and botany pursuits, with good result. In addition to earning
a comfortable living as a merchant, Rafinesque also gained a reputation as one of the pioneer naturalists in America. Thomas Jefferson is
said to have offered him the position of "official botanist" of the Lewis
and Clark Expedition, but Rafinesque declined the position. Instead,
in 1805, he moved to Palmero, Sicily. There he would continue his
scholarly pursuits, writing the first of what would become 950 scien-
tific publications.

However, in 1815 Rafinesque sailed once more for America and
returned to his business ventures, earning what he later described as a
"small fortune" in banking in Philadelphia. This financial security
allowed him to retire from the business world and to devote his whole
life to the study of nature and botany.

In 1818, Rafinesque, at the request of his old friend and business
associate John Clifford, came to Kentucky in order to secure a teach-

ing position at Transylvania College. Clifford, who had worked with Rafinesque in Philadelphia and shared his passion for natural science, had moved to Lexington a few years before and was a trustee of Transylvania College. With Clifford's intercession, college president Horace Holley gave Rafinesque an unsalaried position as professor of natural history and botany at the university.

While this position suited Rafinesque's ambitions nicely, his time at Transylvania was not an easy one. When he began teaching classes at Transylvania University in the fall of 1818, he quickly gained a reputation as a brilliant but thoroughly eccentric instructor. As one college historian put it, "Along with his sterling academic credentials and additions to the science of the time, Rafinesque was noted for his eccentricities—his unpredictable behavior, his careless research and his paranoia." While a scholarly and erudite lecturer, it was for his often erratic behavior that Rafinesque was known. In personal conversation, he was reserved and often abrupt. Although he circulated at social gatherings in Lexington and was even noted as a excellent dancer, he never seemed interested in making social connections with those around him.

In the classroom, Rafinesque was known as brilliant, although less than exacting in his research. His research methods were called sloppy, and although he collected literally thousands of specimens of plant and animal life, little effort was made to preserve or catalogue these samples for posterity. Often he held his classes in the woods surrounding Lexington, a practice that was frowned upon by university officials at the time. Moreover, within his first year at the university, Rafinesque began to make frequent unscheduled forays into the Kentucky wilderness on foot, sometimes for weeks at a time, to study nature and gather specimens. This practice brought him into open conflict with university leadership, and in particular with President Horace Holley.

Despite his great academic achievements, Rafinesque's eccentricities won him few friends among the university community. Students began to refer to Rafinesque as the "Mad Botanist" of the university and he began to find himself shunned by his fellow professors who considered him an "odd fish." Eventually, Rafinesque tired of the friction that was rapidly developing between himself and the university. He felt, with some justification, that the natural sciences did not receive their due respect as a part of the university curriculum. Similarly, Rafinesque made it known he was offended that he was not afforded the honor he felt should have been given a man of his intellectual stature.

With the passing of time, tensions between Rafinesque and the university leadership, particularly President Holley, grew unmanageable. The breaking point came one day when Rafinesque, returning from one of his forays, discovered the president had taken over one of the rooms in which Rafinesque had been staying. As Rafinesque later wrote of the event in his autobiography, *A Life of Travels:*

> To evidence his hatred against sciences and discoveries, he [Holley] had broken open my rooms, given one to the students and thrown all my effects, books and collections in a heap in another room. I took lodgings in town and carried there all my effects.

Thus ended Rafinesque's tenure with Transylvania University.

At the time, the reason given for his dismissal from the university was "unprofessional conduct." However, a rumor in the university hinted at a more dramatic reason. It was said that Rafinesque was conducting an "affair of the heart" with no less a personage than the wife of the university president. While no official confirmation could be found for such a charge, it was noted that Mrs. Holley had been kinder to Rafinesque than most at the school and that he, in turn, had written poetry in her honor.

Whatever the reason for his unceremonious departure, Rafinesque, characteristically, did not take his leave quietly. Instead, it is told that when he departed from campus, he placed a curse on Holley and the university in general. According to a recent article in the student newspaper, Rafinesque, facing Holley at the time of his dismissal, is said to have vowed, "Damn thee and thy school as I place curses upon you."

Although this exact wording is of dubious historical veracity, Rafinesque himself noted the curse in his memoirs of the event:

> Thus leaving the college and curses on it and Holley; who were both reached by them soon after; since he died next year at sea of the yellow fever, caught in New Orleans, having been driven from Lexington by

public opinion; and the college has been burnt in 1828, with all its contents. Time renders justice to all.

While some may debate the efficacy of whatever curse Rafinesque may have leveled at his nemesis, it is true that President Holley was indeed forced from office within a year due to his liberal religious views. Journeying to New Orleans, he contracted yellow fever and died a short time later.

Then in 1828 a servant polishing a student's boots late one night knocked over a candle and caused a fire which destroyed the main hall of campus. Noted at the time, the only articles to escape the destruction were a few papers and belongings that had been left behind by Rafinesque.

As sad as the fate of President Holley might be, Rafinesque himself was not blessed with a happy existence after leaving the university. After departing from Lexington, Rafinesque drifted for a time, eventually spending the rest of his life in Philadelphia, where he died alone and penniless. So dire were his were his financial straits that, had not his physician intervened, his body would have been sold for medical research by an angry landlord. In what he no doubt would have considered a final humiliation, the great Rafinesque was buried in a mass grave in a pauper's cemetery in Philadelphia.

However, this was not to be the end of the troubled bond between Rafinesque and Transylvania University. In 1924, a fund was collected by students and alumni of the college to exhume the body of Rafinesque and place it in a crypt in Old Morrison Hall on the campus grounds. The new crypt prepared, the body was duly raised from the pauper's grave and transported to Lexington. It was laid to rest beneath a marble slab with the words, "Honor to Whom Honor Is Overdue" adorning the door to the crypt.

During the ceremony held to commemorate Rafinesque's return to Transylvania, it was said that this effort was undertaken to give the noteworthy naturalist an honorable burial. However, even then, it was whispered that the reburial was an effort to lift the curse he had placed on the university. For, according to legend, even though Rafinesque left Transylvania University more than a century ago, his curse has remained. As a student reporter noted in 1951, "Since the departure of Rafinesque, many unusual and mysterious things have happened under most peculiar circumstances at Transylvania University."

In addition to the fate of President Holley and the destruction by fire of the main building of the campus in 1824, other devastating events have occurred. According to the stories, a strange tragedy occurs on campus roughly every seven years as a result of the Rafinesque curse.

A few years after the great fire of 1824, a cholera epidemic swept through campus. While such contagions were common at the time, it was noted that this particular epidemic hit the campus just as efforts began to rebuild the building that had been destroyed in the fire. In fact, the rebuilding efforts had to be delayed several months because of the sickness.

If the return of Rafinesque to Transylvania University was an effort to lift his curse, it seems to have done little good. Unexplained and sometimes tragic events have continued to occur in recent years. In late 1961, a young coed was found strangled to death in her car, which happened to be parked just a few hundred feet from the tomb of Rafinesque. Then, in 1969, Old Morrison burned to the ground. Interestingly, the only area of the building not to be destroyed was the crypt of Constantine Rafinesque.

This latter event gave rise to one of the more intriguing aspects of the Rafinesque legend. The story goes that during the fire, two firefighters, while combing the flaming building for victims still inside, entered the precincts of the crypt. What they saw startled them. Although the fire raged all throughout the area, it was said to have stopped short directly before the door of the crypt, as though held back by an invisible wall. As if this were not strange enough, upon looking into the chamber, the firemen were confronted by the vaporous specter of a man standing directly in front of Rafinesque's crypt. The form was said to have turned toward the men, laughed uproariously at the fire, and then disappeared.

Over the years others have reported seeing a strange shadow or white form in the area of the crypt. Still others have reported glimpsing a hazy figure of a short man with dark, piercing eyes walking the halls of Old Morrison. Inevitably, the figure is said to disappear when approached.

In the succeeding years, other odd events have occurred at Transylvania University. Several years ago, a workman fell to his death while doing maintenance on the roof of the campus gymnasium. Another workman walking the dark halls of Old Morrison late one night is said to have tripped over an object and injured himself. A subsequent search of the hallway he was walking, directly before the Rafinesque crypt, showed nothing that could have caused the fall. Although none of the recent events has been as dramatic as the 1969 fire, all have occurred roughly seven years apart and all were blamed, at least by some, on the curse of Rafinesque.

In succeeding years, the university has begun to take a sort of pride in Rafinesque and his curse. Today, there is even a Rafinesque Society on campus, and each October the university celebrates Rafinesque Day, usually just prior to Halloween. On the evening of that day, students gather for a bonfire and members of the Rafinesque Society, wearing long black robes with a large "R" emblazoned across the front, burn a ceremonial coffin in honor of the long-dead scholar. Several years ago, a reporter dispatched from the local paper to cover the event ventured into the tomb of Rafinesque in the early afternoon. Though he found the iron gates to the crypt area locked tightly, what caught his attention was a hand lettered sign hung over the gates. It read, "Be back at midnight." Underneath was the signature, "C. Rafinesque." Perhaps he had indeed stepped out. In any case, the sign and the tomb it decorated serve as a grim reminder of the enigmatic professor and the legacy of his fateful curse.

5
The Faceless Nun of Foley Hall
St. Mary of the Woods College
Terre Haute, Indiana

Should old acquaintance be forgot,
Or pass beyond recall?
Our hearts say no, so kudos go,
to dear old Foley Hall.

I lived in Foley in my youth
(the dates I can't recall)
And I for one
knew growth and fun
in stately Foley Hall.

And every person at these woods,
From greatest to the small
Has tale to tell
that weave the spell
of famous Foley Hall

The faceless nun,
the attic dark
The spiral staircase tall
The chapel, classrooms. courtyard too
All Part of Foley Hall.

Rosemary Nudd, S.P.: from *Toast to Foley Hall*

For many institutions of higher education, the "campus ghost" has become as much a part of college life as the smell of musty library books and ivy clinging to granite walls. Such is the case with St. Mary of the Woods College, a Roman Catholic women's school near Terre Haute, Indiana.

The roots of St. Mary of the Woods can be traced back to 1840, when Mother Theodore Guerin, S.P. (Sisters of Providence) and five other nuns left their mother house in Ruille sur Loir, France, to venture across the Atlantic. Eventually their journey ended in the wilderness of what is now central Indiana, near a small settlement on the banks of the Wabash known as Thrall's Station. Through cold Midwestern winters and hot summers, these dauntless women worked to bring culture and religion to the wilderness.

Eventually a Catholic mission was founded in a wooded glen not far from town. Shortly thereafter, a religious community began to take shape, and in 1846 the first Catholic women's college in the United States was founded. Despite the rural nature of the surroundings, the concept of higher education for women quickly caught on, and by 1860 the college had grown to the point that a more permanent structure was needed to house the school and its inhabitants.

That year the foundation was laid for what would ultimately become a massive structure, called at first " St. Mary's Academic Institute." Later, as the college grew, so did its central edifice, renamed "Foley Hall" after one of the superior generals of the Sisters of Providence.

The next 130 years would see amazing changes at "The Woods" as it has affectionately become known. From its rustic beginnings, St. Mary of the Woods would evolve into a graceful campus of tree-lined streets, wooded vistas, and numerous buildings, most of them reminiscent of European architectural styles.

But it was always Foley Hall that seemed to dominate the campus community. Surrounded on all sides by buildings of lesser stature and history, Foley Hall became the *grande dame* of the college—an institution, it seemed, unto itself. In its time, this Gothic structure would serve its college as dormitory, classroom facility, chapel, infirmary, cafeteria, and even an art studio. With its austere sense of quiet grace and elegance, Foley came to serve as the centerpiece of the college and surrounding community. Generations of women came to her doors for learning and growth, and each in turn left her, promising never to forget the time spent there.

The original cornerstone of Foley Hall, laid in 1860, bore the inscription, "Wisdom hath built herself a house." Judging from the ranks of women who passed through her halls, it seems fair to say that wisdom did indeed reside within her stone walls. However, if the legends surrounding this beloved structure are to be believed, so did something else. Something darker, and more mysterious. Something at once pitiful, yet also sinister—anonymous, nameless, and, quite literally, faceless.

In truth, no one knows the real origin of the legends surrounding the faceless nun, as she came to be known. However, most indications point back to the early part of this century, when Foley Hall was being used primarily as a classroom facility, with a substantial part of the second floor occupied by an art studio. The tale is whispered that a young novitiate came to work there as an art instructor. An accomplished artist herself, this young woman whiled away her free time doing portraits of her fellow sisters. So renowned were her artistic endeavors that it was eventually suggested she attempt an artist's greatest challenge: a self portrait.

Soon the work was begun. As many artists do, she began her work by painting what she could readily see—the blue drape that would form the backdrop of the painting; then slowly her clothes and shape took form. Since the face was the most critical and most difficult aspect of the work, it was reserved for last.

So great was the challenge of this endeavor that soon the artist become consumed with her work. Late into the night she would paint by gas light and shadow. Often the morning would find her slumped in a chair in the second-floor studio, sound asleep, her paintbrush still in hand. As days grew into weeks the painting continued to take shape, but still the face remained untouched—waiting, it seemed, until the last moment.

Then tragedy suddenly intervened. Before the first feature of the face had been put to canvas, the young nun was struck down with a debilitating illness. Perhaps it was one of the many contagions that swept through the countryside in the early 1900s. Perhaps it was simply the strain of long days and nights in the art studio finally taking their toll, but whatever the case, the young woman was found one morning collapsed before her faceless work.

She was carried downstairs to the infirmary, but despite the best ministrations of her fellow sisters, she died a few days later. Death had intervened before she had been able to complete her greatest work by the addition of her face. Her body was quietly interred the next day in the private burial ground on campus. The unfinished painting was moved to a storeroom adjacent to the second-story art loft, leaving only paint spatters and dust behind . . . and, perhaps, if the legends told are true, an unquiet spirit with unfinished business at Foley Hall.

Although, through the years, any number of people have claimed encounters with the faceless nun, the best documented experiences came from Sister Esther Newport, who taught in the art department from 1931 to 1964. Although Sister Esther has been deceased for a number of years, she did relate some of her encounters with the faceless nun to Dawn Tomaszewski, a student reporter for *The Woods,* the campus newspaper.

In this article, Sister Esther recounts a number of experiences she had over many years. The first hint of "trouble" at Foley, she recalled, came late one cold night, when she was working in a small room on the second floor of the building. She knew she was not alone in the building that night; working in the art studio to the rear of the second floor was a girl named Isabel, who was finishing an art project. As the hour grew late, Sister Esther decided to check on Isabel's progress. Quietly she made her way down the long hall that led to the art studio and was shocked to find Isabel standing outside the doorway of the art studio. Sensing that something was wrong, Sister Esther asked the girl what the matter was.

"I'm sick and tired of that nun coming around" replied Isabel, visibly agitated. Thinking it strange that another sister could be in the building without her knowledge, Sister Esther asked Isabel to describe the nun in question. "I don't know," Isabel replied. "She always stands between me and the light—not only that, but she leaves when I try to speak to her and I can never see her face."

Curious as her experience was, this was not be the last time that Isabel would encounter the enigmatic figure. Several weeks later, Sister Esther entered the art studio to find Isabel working on a watercolor project. "Did you find the nun that was looking for you?" Isabel inquired. "She was here just a minute ago." Puzzled, Sister Esther replied that she had seen none of her fellow sisters in the building.

Thus was born the legend of the faceless nun. While the student Isabel was the first person to encounter the phantom of Foley Hall, she was by no means the last. Soon other students began to report strange confrontations with the mysterious presence. One morning Sister Esther met two more female students in the second floor art gallery who reported glimpsing the silent figure of a nun gliding through the room. Assuming that the woman must be looking for Sister Esther, the two sought her out and reported that "a strange nun is looking for you." Again perplexed as to who the anonymous sister might be, Sister Esther asked about her appearance. At first the girls seemed reluctant to describe her, haltingly commenting that the sister had pleats down the front of her dress, in the manner of nuns from a number of years before. When pressed about her appearance further, the girls grew more reticent, until one of the girls, Catherine, blurted out, "You are going to think that I am crazy, sister, but she didn't have no face."

When the first two incidents with Isabel had occurred, Sister Esther had been inclined to write the entire problem off as one student with an overactive imagination. Now, however, she began to suspect that something more inexplicable might be occurring. This feeling was reinforced several weeks later during a figure drawing class that Sister Esther was teaching in the studio. As she sat in one corner of the room, silently observing her students' work on their sketches, she was started to see a girl on the far side of the room look toward the windows and apparently begin talking to thin air. Not knowing quite what to think, Sister Esther approached her from behind and asked her if there was a problem she could help with. At the sound of Sister Esther's voice, the student, a girl named Celine, jumped visibly and said, "But Sister, what are you doing there? You were right next to me a moment ago!"

The next incident occurred about a week later, during the very same class period. In the midst of a lecture, Sister Esther found her words interrupted by a loud "swishing" sound coming from the floor. So loud was this sound that it became impossible to continue her lecture. As one of the girls in the class would tell her granddaughter years afterward, "We all though it sounded different—but for me, it sounded exactly like someone was sweeping the floor with one of those big straw brooms we used to use at home." After much speculation, the class decided that the noise must be originating from some plaster repairs being done on the ceiling of the classroom below. Later investigation, however, revealed that no such repairs were under way in the building.

Such experiences were far too interesting to be kept secret for long on a college campus. Soon the stories of the faceless nun were sweeping through the campus and surrounding community. Much to Sister Esther's surprise, other members of the college began to report previous encounters in Foley Hall. One sister whom Sister Esther describes as a "stolid German nun from Jasper" reported being disturbed several times while she was working in the studio by phantom footsteps approaching her from behind. Finally, the unperturbed sister rather testily told the spirit, "Go away and don't bother me—I'm busy." Perhaps something in her authoritative demeanor might have intimidated even a spirit, for the footsteps disturbed her work no more that night.

An even stranger occurrence happened one night when Sister Esther and a friend were alone in the lofty old studio. Sister Esther, it seems, had been engaged for some time doing the illustrations for a children's Bible and her friend, who worked for a publishing firm in Chicago, had come to review the illustrations. As they looked at the canvases that were finished, Sister Esther walked behind a large painting in order to turn it so that her friend could see the work. Looking up, she was surprised to see that her friend had turned her back to her and was talking to someone—or something—that Esther could not see. Sister Esther, by now aware of what might be happening, spoke gently to the woman, who immediately jumped and turned full circle to face her. "Are you all over this place? You were just in the corner!"

Sister Esther tried to comfort the visibly shaken woman and the two sat down to discuss what was had happened. The question of shadows was dismissed, since a thousand-watt fixture flooded the room with harsh light. As the two sat and spoke about the strange vision, suddenly the woman gasped and pointed in the direction of the painting Sister Esther had just turned around. "Why, there she is again," said the woman. "There is the sister I saw before." Perplexed, Sister Esther watched the woman's finger as it followed an unseen presence from the center of the room into a supply closet where, the woman said, the figure simply "melted into the doorway."

Strange as the incident seems, it looms even more remarkable in light of further discoveries at Foley. Years later, the walls of the art room supply closet were ripped down, and the remains of a stairway were found that once had linked that part of the building with the lower section, where the nuns had once been housed.

By now the rumors sweeping the campus had turned ominous. Students began to avoid classes held in the building and refused to come to the facility at night. Sister Esther, sensing that something should be done, arranged to have a mass said in the chapel, "for special intentions," which were, in truth, to quiet the unruly specter that had taken up residence in Foley Hall. After the mass was said, the spirit seemed to quiet somewhat, but all throughout the proceeding years, girls venturing into the building would report catching a fleeting glimpse of a strange sister in the garb of long ago.

In 1987, Foley Hall was leveled in order to make room for a more modern classroom facility. With her went 147 years of history, tradition, and pride. But who knows that there might also have gone the unquiet spirit of a young nun, who had lost her identity nearly a century before at stately Foley Hall.

6
The Spectral Cadet of West Point
The United States Military Academy
West Point, New York

*But now comes on with veteran pride and far-preceding heralds of
acclaim, the division which knows something of the transmigration of souls:
Having lived and moved in different bodies and under different names . . .*
Major General Joshua Chamberlin

It remains as one of the most extraordinary and controversial epi-
sodes in the annals of American ghostlore. Starting with an incident
as seemingly innocuous as the mysterious movement of a bathrobe
hanging on a shower hook, it grew to captivate the imagination of a
nation for a brief time. Even today, the strange events that occurred in
room 4714 of the 47th Division Barracks at West Point in October
1972 elicit excited debate among the individuals and institutions involved. For some, the incidents provide some of the most well documented evidence of paranormal activity ever collected. For others,
they are simply an indication of bizarre interservice rivalry and the
strange effects of mass hysteria. Only one thing is certain: something
distinctly odd did occur within the hallowed halls of the United States
Military Academy at West Point.

To bring up the name of West Point is to immediately conjure
images of a formidable military institution. Military discipline and
bearing are a point of pride in this vaunted institution whose history
of service to its nation stretches back almost two hundred years. Once
labeled "the choosiest college in the United States" by *USA Today,*
the academy is a massive complex serving as home to over forty-four
hundred cadets, as well as twenty-two hundred military personnel and
four thousand civilians. The facility has its own shopping center, el-
ementary school, hospital and arts center. Students, or cadets as they

are known, are divided into military style companies, each belonging to a larger grouping known as a division. Cadets are assigned barracks according to their division and class year.

The idea of an academy to train the best and brightest for America's military was first put forth by George Washington, but it was 1802 before West Point was founded. Since that time, it has graduated a host of military and political leaders, including Presidents Grant and Eisenhower, as well as a plethora of other prominent figures in American history, including Stonewall Jackson, Robert E. Lee, and General Norman Swartzkopf. Even Edgar Allan Poe had a brief but disastrous career as a cadet at West Point. During its time as the training ground for the elite of our nation, the achievements of service and valor associated with this institution have become a part of our American history and tradition. The "Long Gray Line of West Point," as the student body is known, is an indelible part of our nation's military heritage.

Interestingly, despite the rigid military discipline and bearing of the institution, a subculture of folklore and superstition has developed at the institution. For many years it was a well-established tradition that any student flunking mathematics should go to the prominent statue of General Sedwick on campus and spin the spurs of the statue's boots. If the ritual was accomplished at midnight immediately before the final examination, with the hapless student wearing his full dress uniform, then the benevolent spirit of the general was supposed to grant him good luck and hopefully a passing grade.

Other legends attached to West Point, however, are of a less genial and more eerie nature. Tales are told of wrathful spirits and petulant specters, leading some to speculate that the "Long Gray Line" might well harbor some otherworldly constituents among its ranks.

In truth, there are not one but several ghost stories attached to the Military Academy at West Point. One of the most long standing and heralded legends centers around the home of the academy superintendent, which sits majestically on the campus grounds overlooking the Hudson River.

The home of the superintendent of West Point has been called "a small gem of Federal style." Surrounded by an iron filigree porch with cannons appointing either side, the home seems a serene and stately dwelling. Built in 1820 for West Point's fourth superintendent, Sylvanaus Thayer, the building has been the home of such illustrious personages as Robert E. Lee, Douglas MacArthur, and General William C. Westmoreland. Over the passing years, statesmen and leaders from across the world have been entertained within its walls. About ten thousand guests a year visit the home, including a host of notables from royalty to presidents.

Inside the home, visitors are treated to a rich conglomeration of antique furnishings, all with their own histories, such as a table once belonging to the Lincoln White House and a writing desk belonging to Robert E. Lee. The first floor of the building is devoted to dining and reception space. The superintendent and his family reside in a three-room suite in the second floor living quarters, while the third floor is devoted to guest rooms and storage space. A small basement, once used as sleeping quarters for servants, completes the structure.

This lattermost room has been the basis for the first odd occurrence noted in the home. In the basement area, which is now largely used for storage, there is a small bedroom where, years ago, the house cook was quartered. So tiny is this compartment that there is room only for an antique bed and dresser. Though the room is never used for visitors today, the custom of the household staff is to keep linens on the bed to preserve the room's historic ambience.

Under normal conditions, such a custom would be little noted or appreciated. However, in this case, the carefully made bed linens seem to have attracted the attention of something otherworldly. LuDelia Palmer, wife of General David Palmer, former West Point superintendent, reported to *Hudson Valley* magazine in 1988 that, during her husband's tenure at the academy, she frequently noted something strange about the bed. On her occasional visits to the downstairs bedroom, she noticed that, while the entrance door to the bedroom had been kept locked, she frequently found the bed covers disturbed, as though some had been lying on them. She reported that though she always took care to carefully smooth and remake the bed and then relocked the room when she left, when she returned she would invariably find them ruffled again. "It is as if someone had sat down on the edge of the bed to put his boots on," she told the magazine.

This strange circumstance has given rise to the speculation that the spirit of a former staff member at the house had returned to its place of employment. While no identity may be established for the specter, the legend suggests that the spirit is that of superintendent Sylvanaus Thayer's cook Molly, a high-spirited Irishwoman who was said to have dominated the household. Her spirit is also blamed for a recurrent damp spot in the basement kitchen that no one is able to dry, no matter what means are employed.

Legends surrounding the home also mention a second female apparition in the dwelling. One of the house's previous occupants is said to have seen a lady in white disappear through a door into one of the upstairs bedrooms. "The nicest theory is that the ghost is Abigail Thayer, Sylvanaus's sister," Mrs. Palmer told *Hudson Valley*. "Because Thayer wouldn't allow her to cook in the kitchen, she's paying him back for all eternity."

Other spirits are said to reside on the magnificent academy grounds as well. Old Morrison House, nearby on professor's row, is said to be haunted by the ghost of woman who died in a third floor bedroom there. Rumors of her appearance recurred for many years around campus, though many pragmatic army staff members scoff at such an idea. However, at least one such doubter is said to have been taught a stern lesson by the ghost.

According to the tale, in the 1920s one Captain Bellinger, a doubter of things supernatural, moved into the house. At the time of his residence in the home, he found that the third floor bedroom had been left vacant in deference to the phantom. Unimpressed and undaunted by the idea of sharing his dwelling with a ghost, Captain Bellinger promptly moved two servant girls into the room, being careful not to tell them of the room's haunted reputation. During the very first night there, the women are said to have run screaming from the house when a hazy figure in white floated through their room glaring at them. It is carefully noted that the pair apparently ran into the street wearing only their night clothes, creating a stir on the campus grounds.

Since such goings on were frowned upon by West Point officials, Father O'Keefe, then chaplain to West Point, was brought to the house to "pray out the spirit." It is unknown what effect his intercession had, but rumors of spectral activity in Old Morrison House have resurfaced through the years.

Such stories are surely enough to win West Point a place in any registry of campus ghosts. However, they pale in comparison with the mysterious events that took place in 47th Division Barracks in the fall of 1972 . . . incidents that began inauspiciously, but quickly grew to capture the imagination of the nation and become one of the most well publicized hauntings in American history.

As noted, the episode began innocently. On October 20, Cadet Jim O'Connor, a plebe, or first year cadet, was preparing to take a shower at about at 11:15 P.M. in the common bathroom on the fourth floor of the 47th Division barracks. As O'Connor prepared to enter the shower, he noticed that his bathrobe, which was hanging on a hook on the wall next to the shower, started (in his words) "swinging like a pendulum." At one point, the robe swung to a position almost parallel to the floor and remained there for several seconds, as though held by an unseen force. Then the robe was released from whatever was holding it and returned to its natural position. At the same time, O'Connor noted that the water in the shower had suddenly and inexplicably turned cold. He readjusted the water and glanced back to find the robe had resumed its mysterious swinging motion. At that moment, the water in the shower suddenly turned hot. Find no logical explanation for either phenomena, Cadet O'Connor gave up taking a shower and returned to his room.

Such an experience, strange as it might be, might well have been quickly forgotten were it not for the fantastic occurrences that followed. The next night, O'Connor's roommate, Cadet Victor, was in the same bathroom using the latrine when the urinal he was using flushed before he could put his hand to it. Startled, he turned to see a roll of toilet paper next to an adjacent commode unrolling itself onto the floor.

Remembering his roommate's story of the night before, Victor ran back to his room to get his roommate and together they returned to the bathroom. When they entered, they found the toilet paper completely unrolled onto the floor and the bathroom empty. Now totally perplexed, the pair searched the floor for a prankster but they found they were alone, most of the upperclassmen being on leave for a long weekend.

Things were heating up in the 47th Division barracks and the specter was about to make its first appearance. The incident occurred two nights later, at 1:05 A.M., when O'Connor was again using the latrine. Turning to leave, he noticed someone sitting on the toilet seat to one side of the bathroom. Realizing that no one had been in the room when he entered, the cadet turned and saw a figure that was later described as being about five feet six inches tall, and "dressed in a full dress gray coat." In his official report, Cadet O'Connor later described the figure as sitting stiffly upright, as one would sit on a bench. In its right hand it held a vintage Civil War musket, complete with bayonet.

As though such a figure, sitting serenely on a toilet seat, was not bizarre enough to unnerve the young man, O'Connor later said that what frightened him most were the eyes of the figure. "They were white," he later described, "and they were glowing."

Badly frightened, O'Connor stumbled back to his room and blurted out his story to his roommate. While both of them recognized that they had encountered a strange series of events, they decided to remain quiet about what they had experienced, fearing the ridicule of the upperclassmen and company officers should their story leak out. However, this decision soon became untenable, as the manifestations grew in scope and the phantom cadet left the precincts of the common bathroom.

The next night, O'Connor and Victor were studying in their room when they noticed that the temperature suddenly had grown unnaturally cold. O'Connor looked up and called out to his roommate, "Do you see something?" Turning toward the direction in which his roommate was staring, Cadet Victor felt his breath catch in his throat. Both men later agreed that as they stared in the direction of the room radiator, they saw an indistinct white shape slowly forming itself from thin air and floating between four and five feet from the floor. The vision lasted twenty to thirty seconds, then seemed to evaporate.

Both cadets were now thoroughly shaken, yet still they resolved to remain quiet regarding what was happening around them. However this was not to be the specter's last visit to their room. On October 30, shortly after the nightly playing of taps, the two roommates were again seated in their alcoves on opposite sides of their barracks room. Suddenly they noticed that the temperature in the room had again grown strangely cold. Sensing that something was about to happen, both young men watched carefully. Within a few moments, the by-now-familiar figure of a soldier in the garb of long ago appeared out of the wall above Victor's locker.

The specter, which appeared three dimensional and very real, strolled silently around Victor's alcove as the frightened cadet sat motionless at his desk. After wandering aimlessly for a moment, it disappeared into the wall, only to reemerge a moment later on O'Connor's side of the room. This time, it wandered for a moment, then approached O'Connor directly and suddenly disappeared.

With the disappearance of the apparition, O'Connor once again noted the cold temperature of the room and approached the radiator. He found that, though it was fully on, he could feel no heat unless he actually touched the radiator itself.

Both men now realized that they had to report the inexplicable events to their commanding officer. While incredulous as to the phenomena they reported, Keith Bakken, commanding officer of Company G4, as well as platoon leader Terry Mechan, decided to conduct their own investigation. Cadet Bakken was of the expressed opinion that the entire event was some sort of joke or hoax, but he and Cadet Mechan reluctantly agreed to sleep in the room to see for themselves. Within a few hours they would have reason to doubt both their initial conclusions and to regret their decision to occupy the room.

The two officers later reported in their official statements that they stayed up drinking coffee until about 1:30 A.M. At this point, Mechan again expressed his opinion that the entire episode was a joke and admitted that if there was a specter haunting the room, he did not care to see it. As though on cue, a few moments later the temperature in the room began to drop noticeably. Bakken, rationalizing that it was just his imagination, pulled his woolen blanket over his head and tried in vain to sleep. At about 1:45 A.M. he rolled over onto his back and pulled the blanket down for a moment.

What he saw made him cry out in alarm. He was staring at the head and neck of a man looking down at him from the ceiling of the room. As he later told the West Point newspaper, *The Assembly,* "I just looked up and it was there. It was the three-quarters profile of the head and neck. I could see one eye was blurry. Its nose and mouth were black. This lasted for about two minutes."

The two officers immediately turned on the light in the room and searched it for some means of explaining the image, but none was found. The next morning, after a nearly sleepless night, both men stood on the bed in which Mechan had been lying and looked carefully at the ceiling above, searching for a water stain or spot, but the plaster above was clean and unblemished.

Now convinced, the two men reported the incident to the assistant brigade adjutant, Cadet John Feeley, who, upon hearing the strange tale, decided to sleep in the room himself. That night, he and Cadet O'Connor settled into the room for the night to "test the spirit" again.

As Feeley later related the tale, he noticed nothing out of the ordinary in the room when he entered it and went to sleep about midnight. However, at 2:30 A.M. he woke up suddenly. Though the room once again was very cold, Feeley said he was bathed in sweat. Furthermore, he felt his breathing was being stifled, as though something monstrously heavy was lying on his chest.

Opening his eyes, he saw the image of a man protruding from the wall high above him. He later described the image as wearing a high collar and tall black hat. "I did not notice much besides the eyes," he later reported to *The Assembly*. "Rather than eyes it had white spots. I tried to sit up in bed but could not. I made an effort to scream, but the sound was cut off in my throat."

Hearing choking sounds from the other side of the room, O'Connor jumped to his feet and ran to Feeley's bedside. "He sounded scared," O'Connor later explained. "I guess we both were. I came over and saw the image just as it was going back into the wall." O'Connor described the image as about five feet six inches tall and floating above the bed. Though the room was cold, when the men touched the wall where the form had disappeared, it was colder still.

As word of the strange goings on began to spread, others in the barracks began to volunteer their efforts to investigate the phenomena. Later that week, three cadets on the battalion staff decided to try their hand at sleeping in the room, once more accompanied by Cadet

O'Connor. This time they came prepared, bringing with them a thermocouple capable of measuring nearly instantaneous temperature changes.

This device, which had been purloined form the Earth, Space and Graphic Sciences Department, was to yield some startling results. At one point in the evening, Cadet O'Connor left the room to go to the latrine. Within seconds of his departure, the temperature in the room dropped from its normal 27°C to -18°C. Upon O'Conner's return, the temperature abruptly returned to 27° but a few moments later dropped again to 7°. It shortly rose to normal temperature again, only to drop to 14° again shortly thereafter.

While investigating these unexplained fluctuations in temperature, the men walked around the room with the thermocouple, attempting to locate the source of the cold. Strangely, they found the temperature was always lowest in the vicinity of Cadet O'Connor. As he moved around the room, the cold spot seemed to follow him.

Following this experiment, the men turned off the lights in the room and lit a candle. It burned evenly for about a minute; then the flame suddenly rose to a height of six inches, where it stayed for about three minutes, until the candle was extinguished.

As word of the startling phenomena began to spread through the barracks and Academy, speculation ran rampant as to the possible identity of the specter. Several cadets, rummaging through the West Point archives, discovered that in the late nineteenth century, an officer assigned to the academy had been burned to death when his home had been gutted by fire. The house in question stood just adjacent to the area where the 47th Division barracks now stands. Another theory at the time stated that the phantom resulted from the 47th Division barracks' proximity to West Point's "Execution Hollow" and cemetery where military prisoners were routinely executed during the last century.

Whatever the identity of the phantom warrior, his presence could no longer be kept under wraps. Interestingly, instead of covering up the situation, the administration of West Point took it seriously and in the first week of November issued a press statement on the matter. Admitting that "unexplained phenomena" were occurring in the room,

Lieutenant Colonol Patrick Dionne, Academy information officer, told the Associated Press that while he was a nonbeliever, "something has happened and we've not been able to explain what it is." Dionne then went to on to add, "There has been a lot of joking going on about the apparition—notice we are not calling it a ghost—but there are many who are taking it very seriously."

Soon a carnival atmosphere began to pervade the room and the Academy itself. Hundreds of reporters trooped through the barracks, and the Academy was deluged by offers of assistance from professional and amateur ghost hunters, all wishing to spend the night in the afflicted room. The story was eventually run in the *New York Times, Time* magazine, *Newsweek, Life,* and UPI, as well as countless other, smaller publications, and broadcast on the BBC, CBS, and NBC.

For a few brief weeks it seemed the attention of the entire nation was captured by the story. So swamped was the superintendent's office with requests for information and access that the West Point administration quickly transferred cadets O'Connor and Victor to other quarters and declared the room off limits to all Academy and civilian personnel.

With the closing of room 4714, the strange incidents that had so plagued the 47th Division barracks ceased, and the story might well have faded from public notice except for an extraordinary and some might say bizarre confession from another military student a few hundred miles away.

On October 29, 1972, Midshipman William Gravell, a senior at the United States Navel Academy in Annapolis, Maryland, held a press conference. To those reporters gathered, Midshipmen Gravell announced that the ghostly escapades at West Point were nothing more than a practical joke perpetrated by Gravell and several other midshipmen to expose the West Point cadets to ridicule. Such interservice pranks are common, particularly between service academies in the days and weeks before their annual football contests. Evidence of this is the fact that just two days prior to Gravell's announcement, the West Point Cadets had announced they had "acquired" the Navy mascot from its home in Annapolis.

Gravell reported that he had paid five or six nocturnal visits to the Army campus, and with the help of another unnamed midshipman, lowered a photographic slide attached to a flashlight from the roof to the window outside room 4714. Cheesecloth, he related, was placed between the flashlight beam and the slide to soften the light. Gravell also reported that in order to heighten the effect, he had placed a fire extinguisher into an air shaft that led from the roof to the room and allowed the carbon dioxide to slowly leak in. In addition to making the room unnaturally cold, it was this CO^2 that produced what he termed "funny little noises. . . I wanted something they wouldn't be able to pin on us, but something that, with the tradition-bound atmosphere of West Point, they would really swallow," Gravell told the press corps. "Well, they fell for it—fell much further than I would have imagined."

Gravell claimed to the press that he had produced the slide by photographing a fellow midshipman in an antique military uniform. Gravell said that he had deliberately underexposed the slide so the picture would have a dim and milky appearance. Reflecting back on the event, Gravell later told the *Philadelphia Inquirer,* "They [the West Point Cadets] just can't take a joke. I'm really surprised at Army's unsportsmanlike attitude. They just didn't take it like they should have."

If Midshipman Gravell was unimpressed with the reaction of the West Point cadets prior to that point, he must have been more taken aback to their response to his announcement. The reaction from West Point and its cadets was direct and to the point. Officials of the Academy greeted his story with suspicion, pointing out its proximity to the announcement of West Point's acquisition of the Navy mascot and hinting that Gravell's story had been made up to redeem the reputation of Navy and steal the limelight from West Point. West Point cadets were even more adamant in their rebuttal of Gravell. "We can prove beyond a shadow of a doubt that he is not telling the truth," said Keith Bakken, one of the cadets who claimed to have seen the ghost.

Indeed, some evidence indicated by the cadets did seem to cast a shadow of doubt on the midshipman's confession. It was pointed out that on several occasions when the image was seen, the windows in the room were covered by drapes, making it unlikely that a slide could have been shone through a window. They also asserted that the heating vent in which Gravell claimed to have placed the fire extinguisher was not accessible from the roof and even had it been accessible, it would have led to all the rooms in the hallway, not just room 4714. Finally, the fact that the specter's first appearance had been in the fourth floor bathroom, where there were no windows through which to shine a slide, was brought forth as further evidence to contradict the Navel Academy story.

For some, the controversy still rages today. If one were to ask a graduate of the Navel Academy about the incident, they would be likely to grin and point to this story as evidence of their institution's superiority in the area of practical jokes and mischief. However, if one inquires of a West Point graduate concerning the ghost of the 47th barracks, a very different reaction is elicited. For those associated with this venerable military institution, the ghost of the 47th barracks is still very real. Whether the product of hoax, fancy, or forces beyond human understanding, the ghostly cadet, like the other phantoms at the United States Military Academy, has his own unique place in the Long Gray Line of West Point.

7

The Ghosts of William and Mary
The College of William and Mary
Williamsburg, Virginia

The boundaries which divide Life from Death are at best shadowy and vague.
Who shall say where one ends and the other begins?

Edgar Allan Poe

If there is one location in America where history literally comes alive, it is Colonial Williamsburg in eastern Virginia. A perfect jewel of antique grace and beauty, the village consists of over fifty buildings that have been carefully and faithfully restored to the splendor that once was this colonial capital. A walk down the cobblestone streets, past characters dressed in eighteenth-century costume, seems to take one back across the centuries and squarely into the pages of American history. The colonial section was painstakingly restored in the 1920s with funds donated by famed philanthropist John D. Rockefeller, Jr. Today, Williamsburg serves as a center of history and commerce, drawing nearly three million tourists and historians each year.

Sitting imperially on the edge of downtown Williamsburg, the College of William and Mary is an American institution unto itself. Founded in 1693, William and Mary has served continually as an institution of higher learning for over three hundred years and has produced many national leaders in government, business and the arts. As the second oldest college in the United States, it fits perfectly with the unique village it abuts. With many buildings dating from the eighteenth and early nineteenth centuries and ancient trees dotting the campus landscape, the school fairly pervades an atmosphere of colonial charm and gentility.

Like the town of Williamsburg itself, the school is rich in history and tradition. Visiting the college today, one cannot escape the impression that William and Mary is a place where past and present are interwoven in a beautiful and delicate balance. Perhaps, as some believe, this might explain why some elements of this history remain active today in ways that defy logic and understanding. For it is said that at this quaint colonial school, so steeped in its great past, revenants of that past still walk.

Much of the ghostly history of William and Mary, Williamsburg and Virginia itself has been carefully chronicled by author L. B. Taylor in a series of fascinating books on the subject. In his *Ghosts of Historic Williamsburg,* Taylor lovingly and exhaustively weaves the spell of the college and its ghostly inhabitants. It is from this work that the most complete narratives of these legends can be drawn, including the tales related in this book.

One notable haunted locale is the college president's home. A substantial three-story brick building featuring a steep roof and tall chimneys, the house has been described by architectural historians as the "perfect Georgian home." Built in Queen Anne style, the graceful residence was designed by noted colonial architect Henry Clay, Jr., who went on to design much of the campus, as well as the impressive Governor's Palace in Williamsburg.

The foundation for the home was laid in July 1732. The college's first president, John Blair, took up residence there in October 1733, and since that time, the residence has served as home to his successors and their families. Significantly, the only time this service was interrupted was in 1781, during the final weeks of the Revolutionary War, when Lord Cornwallis, commander of the British army, set up his temporary headquarters in the home. Shortly thereafter, his military defeat forced Cornwallis to abruptly abandon the home, following which it was taken over by the French General Lafayette, who used the structure as a hospital for his wounded men.

During this period, in December 1781, a fire swept through the building. Most of the wounded men staying in the home at the time escaped the inferno, but much of the interior was totally destroyed. The fire represented a devastating loss, not only for the College of

William and Mary, but for Virginia itself. Funds for the renovation of the building were eventually approved by the King of France, since the building was in use by his countrymen at the time of its destruction. The restoration took about four years to complete.

During its historic tenure as home to twenty-four university presidents and their families, the president's house has hosted a great many important dignitaries: George Washington truly did sleep there, as did Thomas Jefferson, James Madison and John Tyler. U.S. presidents from Warren Harding to Dwight Eisenhower have been entertained within its elegant walls and a host of other historic figures, including Ben Franklin and Patrick Henry, are also said to have visited the home.

Much like the university itself, the remarkable history of this home seems to pervade the very atmosphere of the place today. As Zoe Graves, wife of former college president Thomas Graves, commented to L. B. Taylor, " I just love this place. Just think . . . [of all the people who have been here.] I believe they all left a certain spirit in the house. No house is devoid of spirits once people have been there. Quality of thoughts do remain. I feel we're companions to our predecessors who lived here and to their guests."

This eloquently stated sentiment sums up much of the atmosphere of the home. However, if the old stories are true, something else has left its mark here—something enigmatic and mysterious. One of the recurrent "problems" with the home, as Mrs. Graves pointed out to Taylor, concerned a closet door in an upstairs bedroom. According to an old story, for many years this door constantly remained open, no matter what means were employed to keep it shut. Residents of the house would close the closet door, securing it tightly, only to have it pop open before their eyes. This inexplicable behavior continued until one day some years ago when workmen made a startling discovery. At that time, renovations were being done on the home and workmen were repairing the small crawl space attic above the third floor. As several carpenters crawled through this small area, they found an ancient human skeleton somehow "pressed" into the original brick wall directly above the third floor closet.

Due to the age of the remains, identification of the body was impossible. However, speculation ran wild at the time. Some suggested that perhaps this was one of Lafayette's wounded soldiers whose life had been ended by the fire of 1781. Others proposed the idea that it could be the remains of a servant who had died in the home and whose death, for some reason, had been hidden from the world.

In any case, the bones were painstakingly removed from the home and buried quickly. This would have no doubt have concluded the mysterious incident except for a strange consequence that was later linked to it. In the weeks that followed, it was realized that the very day the bones were removed from the small attic, the closet door, which lay immediately below the place where they had reposed for so many years, ceased its mysterious opening. As one local folklorist has put it, "It is almost as though the removal of the body brought peace to that section of the house."

While this may well be the case, other sections of the home have not been so blessed. It is whispered that another noted spirit also inhabits the house… a restless, sometimes bothersome spirit that has made itself known for over two hundred years. The "ghost of the president's house" is a common legend on campus. "He's supposed to be the spirit of a French soldier who died of his wounds in the house," Mrs. Graves reported to Mr. Taylor. "He died in the small back room on the third floor and the story is he lingers between the second and third floors."

According to the stories told over the years, phantom footsteps have frequently been heard descending the main staircase from the third to the second floors. While Mrs. Graves appears to have been reluctant to attribute these sounds to paranormal sources, her husband was more adamant about something strange in the house. "He is there," President Graves flatly told Mr. Taylor. " I can't hear as well as my wife, so I haven't heard the footsteps, but I have felt a certain presence in the house. There's definitely some form of psychic phenomena involved."

Graves was not the first university president to encounter strange occurrences in the two-hundred-year old home. President Davis Paschall, who lived in the house from 1960 to 1971, also told of encounters with a spectral presence in the home. Dr. Paschall told L. B.

Taylor that he frequently heard footsteps in the house, particularly late at night. "Once my wife and I were awakened around three in the morning by what we believed were steps. It was something on the stairs moving downward. It was very clear to us and it was an unusual feeling. Then it stopped as abruptly as it began."

Nor was this the only time President Paschall and his wife heard strange noises in the their home. "Another time, my wife and I were watching TV in our upstairs bedroom when we distinctly heard the front door close. It's a heavy door and there is no mistaking the sound. We called down to see if our son or daughter had come in. But no one was there. We looked out the back window but no one had left the house. It was a strange sensation."

Although current university president Timothy Sullivan has stated that he has encountered nothing unusual in the house, some believe that the spirit lingers there still. After two hundred years of residence, whatever spirit remains in this genteel home seems to have as much claim to the building as anyone.

While the president's house is perhaps the most famous haunt at William and Mary, other legends abound on campus. Another haunted location is Phi Beta Kappa Hall, which serves as the theater for William and Mary. Here, it is said, a mischievous spirit named "Lucinda" has made her presence known for more than thirty years. One of the first and best known encounters with the spirit occurred one late night over thirty years ago when music student Larry Raiken was alone in the theater rehearsing a piano piece for an upcoming recital. Finishing his practice, he stopped to gather his music in order to leave when he was astonished to hear a female voice clearly call out, "Oh, don't stop!" Startled, as he knew he was alone in the auditorium, Raiken searched the area, turning on lights as he went, only to find that he was indeed alone.

As he entered the scene room below the stage, however, a fuse suddenly blew, plunging him into total darkness. To add to his consternation, exactly at that moment the door by which he had entered inexplicably slammed shut behind him. Raiken spent a terrifying twenty minutes in the blackness as he searched for an exit. Finally finding the door, he made a rapid departure from the building.

This was not to be Raiken's last encounter with the phantom. In 1970, following a concert at the hall, he and fellow student Calvin Remsberg were in the building cleaning up the stage area. Late that night, having finished their work, the pair decided to improvise an opera with Raiken at the piano and Remsberg providing the lyrics. After a few moments, Remsberg's impromptu performance was cut short when he saw what he described as "the figure of a woman dressed in a long black dress and long black veil" float from the stage manager's box to the other side of the stage. Once again, a search of the area provided no clue as to the identity of the intruder.

An even more startling incident was related by former student Wayne Aycock. Aycock relates that one night while a student at William and Mary, he found himself alone in Phi Beta Kappa Hall, sorting music in the orchestra pit. Finishing his work, Aycock opened a door leading out of the pit to take his leave. As he did so, however, what appeared to be electric sparks flew past him through the open door. As though on cue, suddenly eerie music filled the night. Walking toward the sound of the music, Aycock discovered, in a long unused room under the stage, an old pipe organ. Though the instrument had been broken for years, it was playing itself, according to Aycock, who hastily vacated the premises.

Other stories abound. Another student, Anne Chancellor, told the student newspaper, the *Flat Hat,* that one evening as she was working on a stage flat in the middle of the stage, she heard the side stage door open and footsteps quietly approaching her. Though concentrating on her work, she became aware of the feeling that she was being closely scrutinized. Yet when she looked up she realized she was very much alone.

Chancellor also reported another unsettling incident one night when she was in the lighting area adjacent to the projection booth for the theater. Hearing a noise coming from the projection booth, Chancellor turned toward the area, yelling out, "Hey, who is it?" Opening the door between the two rooms, she peered into the darkened chamber and was startled to see what she later described as a white face staring at her from the recesses of the booth. Again asking, "Who is it?" Chancellor flicked on the light. As she did so, the vision vanished and the room was found empty.

Legend has it that this is not the first time strange phenomena have been reported in the vicinity of the lighting booth. According to an article in the *Flat Hat,* years ago during a play rehearsal, another student was sent to the lighting booth to set the sound for a fellow student who was practicing piano. A moment after entering the booth, however, the student was seen making a hasty exit. When she returned to the stage area, a friend noticed her trembling and asked her what had occurred in the booth. The girl replied that as she had opened the door to the lighting area, she had been frightened by the sound of strange laughter echoing out from the projection booth. A subsequent search of the booth found it devoid of human habitation.

Another encounter with the ghostly presence came several years ago after a rehearsal for the musical *Stop 13.* Freshman student Ralph Byers, choreographer for the play, and a friend were standing on stage when they noticed the overhead fixture in the lighting booth suddenly turn on. Looking into the booth, both men clearly saw a woman with long dark hair and a white dress standing by the window looking out at them. Then, as suddenly as it was turned on, the light in the booth was turned off. Keeping their eyes clearly on the booth, the men jumped from the stage and made their way toward the booth. In order to eliminate any chance of the woman escaping unnoticed, each student ran up a separate staircase toward the booth. When they arrived, however, the light was off and the room was vacant.

Inevitably, as the story of the ghost of Phi Beta Kappa Hall began to spread, students began to filter into the building in an attempt to communicate with whatever spirit might reside there. In the late 1960s, Jeff Rockwell and two friends stayed in the building after a play rehearsal one night on just such a mission. Turning out all of the lights in the theater, the three sat in silence at the edge of the stage to await the phantom lady's appearance.

As it happened, they would not wait in vain. While the elusive specter chose not to show herself that night, at least visually, the students later claimed that she did make her presence known. As they sat amid the darkness of the auditorium expanse, suddenly a rush of cold air breezed up to them from the orchestra pit below and seemed to cling to them. A musty smell, which one of the students later described as "the odor of dark crypts" engulfed them and seemed to follow them as they quickly rose and ran from the stage.

Perhaps the most baffling and eerie of the manifestations at Phi Beta Kappa Hall centers around a wedding dress used as a costume for plays there. The tale is told that many years ago the dress was to have been worn by a young actress in a play at the theater. However, shortly before opening night, the actress was killed in a tragic accident.

As the saying goes, "the show must go on" and an understudy was asked to take the unfortunate girl's place. However, the newly deceased actress had perhaps retained some claim to her former role. On the evening before opening night, the replacement actress was on stage rehearsing lines to herself and could not escape the feeling that she was not alone in the theater. There seemed to be a presence, at once ominous and somehow sad, pervading the very air around her. Finally, something in the auditorium itself attracted her attention. Squinting into the dim recess of the auditorium, she gasped. There, sitting upright in a seat in the third row, was the wedding dress she was to wear the next night. She is said to have reported, "It looked as though it was sitting there listening to me!"

In fact, this fated wedding dress was to play a part in a number of other baffling occurrences in the theater. On another occasion the campus police, on a routine check of the building after hours, are said to have been temporarily blinded by a spotlight turning itself on and aiming itself directly at their faces. Racing to the catwalks high above the auditorium, they found the same wedding dress, neatly folded and lying on a chair next to the spotlight in question. The tale goes on to say that a strange sound then lured them through the building for an hour that night, always keeping just out of the reach of their flashlight beams. Eventually, the security officers left the building in bewilderment.

Others strange reports are whispered about the old theater. It is said that the sound of a woman's soft laugh has occasionally been heard floating through the vacant building late at night. Others report glimpsing a hazy white figure way making its way through the auditorium at odd hours. In truth, the identity of this apparition has never been established, yet belief in her presence runs strong among the

THE GHOSTS OF WILLIAM & MARY 73

theater students at William and Mary. "We believe it," says one theater major. "You try not to think about it while you are in the theater
at night but when something goes bump, we know Lucinda is around
somewhere."

The ghost of the president's house and the famed Lucinda of Phi
Beta Kappa Hall are but two of the shades said to haunt the beautiful
campus of William and Mary. However, according to campus lore,
they are by no means the only such haunts. Another whole genre of
haunted tales center around a unique chapter in the school's history
and the enigmatic spirit of an Indian brave who is said to still seek the
freedom stripped from him over 250 years ago.

It is both ironic and apropos that the athletic teams fielded by
William and Mary bear the name "the Indians." Apropos because
Native Americans played a brief but significant part in the history of
the university, and ironic because the tale is so sad. When the College
of William and Mary was still new, Native Americans were common
in the woods and hills surrounding the budding colony of
Williamsburg. The history of the relationship between settlers and
Indians in Virginia is an unsettled one. Periods of good will and coop-
eration were permeated by intervals of conflict and bloodshed.

Finally, in the late seventeenth century, when both the college
and the colony were in their infancy, a new school was established in
Williamsburg, housed on the grounds of William and Mary. Called
the Brafferton School, the purpose of this institution was to take young
Indian boys and "civilize them" by teaching them the English language and the intricacies of colonial culture. At the time, it was thought
that by training these men and then allowing them to return to their
tribes, better relations could be built between the colony and Virginia's
original inhabitants. It was also thought that by teaching these young
men the fundamentals of the Christian faith, eventually the Indian
nation might be Christianized.

However noble the motivations for this experiment might have
been, in truth it proved a harsh, difficult life for the young Native
Americans involved. These young men, many of whom were taken
against their will from their tribes and settlements, were forced to
trade the freedom of their natural way of life for long hours of study

in a crowded building not far from the center of town. To make matters more difficult, when not studying the boys were housed with local farmers and townspeople, many of whom were distrustful of their
dark-skinned wards. More disastrous still was the fact that the young
men were fed a diet consisting mainly of pork and corn meal. Many
of the young men, unused to such a diet, contracted tuberculosis from
the tainted pork and died. Others, heartbroken and psychologically
unprepared for their rude introduction into a foreign culture, simply
withered away and died of other causes.

Finally, an attempt was made to better the condition of the young
men. A large brick building was erected on the campus of William
and Mary, called the Brafferton Building. Large and airy, this spacious new building served as dormitory and classroom facility for the
boys. It was hoped that by bringing the young men together to live
and study, the morale problem so prominent among them could be
bettered. At first this did seem to be the case, particularly under the
benevolent guidance of a new headmaster named Mr. Griffin. In the
beginning, the young men seemed to be healthier and at least a little
happier. However, this reprieve proved only temporary. After the
untimely death of Mr. Griffin a few months later, conditions worsened again and the building was once more filled with broken-spir-
ited, melancholy young men.

With the passing of time, it became apparent to all concerned that
the Brafferton School experiment was a failure. In 1736, the Brafferton
School for Indians was abandoned and the young men involved were
allowed to return to their tribes and families. However, this sad and
unsuccessful experience in education seems to have left a strange
legacy at William and Mary. At least two ghostly legends have sprung
up around this bit of history. One centers on the Brafferton Building
itself (which still stands on campus), and an even stranger story re-
gards the spirit of one particular Indian boy who, it is said, has never
left the grounds of William and Mary.

Today the Brafferton Building serves as offices for the university
president and the provost. Over the years it has managed to acquire a
strange and somewhat sinister reputation. Rumors have recurred of
strange events and inexplicable sounds emanating from the place at

odd hours of the day and night. Consequently, students and even faculty are said to avoid the building after nightfall.

In *The Ghosts of Old Williamsburg,* L. B. Taylor recounts the experiences of Wilford Kale, the longtime Williamsburg bureau chief for the *Richmond Times Dispatch.* During the mid 1960s, years before he began his work with the newspaper, Kale worked for a summer at William and Mary College and lived on the third floor of Brafferton, where the young Indian men had slept two centuries before. Kale told Taylor, "I definitely heard sounds that summer which you could describe as psychic phenomena, or whatever you want to call it. I know they didn't come from any known source because I couldn't find any explanation for them." On several occasions, Kale reported the sound of phantom footsteps echoing through the third floor of the building where the Native American men had once lived. "The sound was very clear," he recalled. "It was someone walking around. It wasn't a shutter banging or boards creaking. Each time, I got up to look, but I never saw anything."

The incident that seemed to shake Kale the most occurred one night when he awoke from a sound sleep to hear the sound of Indian tom toms echoing through the empty building. "I was awakened by this rhythmic beat on drums. I sat straight up in bed. It must have gone on for a minute and a half. I got up and walked into the hallway. Then I walked down to the first floor and back up again but I saw nothing. It was a spooky feeling."

Others, too, are rumored to have encountered unearthly sounds emanating from the third floor of the Brafferton Building. Many have speculated that such phenomena are in some way linked to the young Native Americans who once lived so unhappily within the walls of the building. If indeed this is the case, then the occurrences in the old building are just a part of the ghostly legacy left to the school by these hapless young men. Another supernatural campus story that has been handed down for generations centers on one of these young men who, it is said, wanders the campus grounds searching for a freedom he has never found.

During the darkest days of the Brafferton School experiment, one young Indian is said to have sought and found a source of escape from the rigors of the school, if only for a short period of time each day. Like many young men at the school, this young brave had been orphaned by one of the skirmishes between settlers and Native Americans. Realizing he had no home to return to, the young man determined to make the best of his existence with the white men. Still, with the passing of time, he yearned for the freedom of his former life. Eventually, his hunger for freedom turning to desperation, he discovered a way to fulfill his need for freedom, if only for a few hours each night.

Though the building was carefully locked at sunset each evening to prevent escape, the young man discovered a way to liberation. It is said that each night, after the lamps were extinguished, he would don his traditional loincloth and climb out a third floor window with the aid of a rope ladder he had secreted away. It was his time to enjoy a sweet but brief taste of precious liberty. A naturally gifted runner, the young man would fly through the night on the wooded grounds of the campus. Those who reported catching a glimpse of him said that he ran with a remarkable grace and agility. Acquiring the endurance of a long-distance runner, he would run for hours, often returning, exhausted, to his bed at daybreak. It was an invaluable escape from the confines of the society into which he had found himself thrust

Soon, however, word spread concerning this elusive boy and his nocturnal forays. Townspeople began to whisper uncomfortably about a young Indian boy loose at night, running through the campus. Yet, since no one was able to actually catch him, his identity could not be proven.

As sweet as these fleeting periods of freedom were for the boy, they were not to last. One morning his crumpled form was found along one of his favorite footpaths. The cause of his death cannot be ascertained with certainty. Today some say it was exhaustion from long days of study and long nights of running free. At the time, others whispered that he had been shot by local townspeople lying in ambush for him. Whatever the case, the boy was quietly interred and his story forgotten, or so it seemed.

On the contrary, it is said that the courageous spirit of this fleet-footed Indian brave has remained. Throughout the succeeding decades and centuries, many students have reported catching a glimpse of a nearly naked young man running through the night along the paths on campus. Students walking home after late night gatherings have encountered him rushing past them among the tree-lined lanes and pathways. In the mid 1970s a campus security officer is said to have encountered him early one misty spring morning and given chase, only to have the figure seemingly evaporate in the mist before his startled eyes.

One rainy spring evening in the mid 1980s, three William and Mary coeds were returning to their dorm from an evening lecture. As the trio made their way among the ancient trees, they became aware of a figure rapidly approaching them out of the darkness. Without thought, the three girls stepped off the path to allow the figure to pass and as they did so, their surprise turned to outright shock. As one girl later reported, "What we saw was a man stripped to the waist. It was dark and we could not see his features clearly, but it looked to me like he had long hair and some sort of leggings on. He passed by really fast and it was not till he was gone that we all sort of realized that when he ran past us his feet had made no sound on the path. We ran back to the dorm that night and locked our doors."

While this story is open to interpretation, still the legend of the young Indian brave continues, as do all of the ghostly legends attached to this venerable institution. While the incredulous may scoff, still the legends serve as a link with the vast history of William and Mary. They serve as a reminder that in this unique place, history literally walks.

8

Millikin's Ghosts
Millikin University
Decatur, Illinois

From Ghoulies and Ghosties and Long Legged Beasties and things that go bump in the night, may the good Lord save us.

Old Gaelic Prayer

The archives department of one large Midwestern college, when queried as to whether there was any ghostlore attached to the campus, replied somewhat contemptuously, "Sorry, but we do not believe in ghosts here. We are a ghost free zone." This seemed like a somewhat odd reply until an alumni of the university, hearing the comment explained, "You have to understand that this is an engineering school. Everybody knows we engineers have no souls, and hence there can be no ghosts." While his fellow engineers might deny this, it is true that some college campuses simply do not lend themselves to ghostlore.

On the other hand, some campuses seem to so prone to the supernatural that they spawn not one, but several ghost stories. Such is the case with Millikin University in Decatur, Illinois. An austere, turn-of-the-century college campus, Millikin is said to be haunted by a myriad of ghostly presences.

This is according to Troy Taylor, who has carefully cataloged the spirits of Millikin in his exhaustive and fascinating book, *The Ghosts of Millikin University.* Taylor, president and founder of the American Ghost Society, has written three books on the ghosts of Decatur. In explaining why Millikin University should host such an abundance of spirits, Taylor simply states that Millikin is located in Decatur, which "probably has more ghosts, haunted spots and eerie legends than anyplace outside of Chicago."

Millikin University was the brainchild of Decatur businessman and philanthropist James Millikin. Born in 1827 in Clarkstown, Pennsylvania, Millikin grew up as the son of a farmer of moderate means. Educated during his formative years in a one-room schoolhouse, Millikin eventually attended Washington University to study business. While at Washington, Millikin took note of the struggle of many of his fellow students to obtain money for college college and resolved that, "should he ever be able to make his fortune, he would create his own college that all classes of people could afford to attend."

The process of acquiring his fortune began for Millikin in the summer of 1849 when, while still a college student, he convinced his father to help him drive a flock of sheep from Pennsylvania to Indiana, where they sold the livestock at a good profit. Over the next several springs, the pair repeated the process with ever-larger numbers of livestock, each time increasing their profits. By the time Millikin was in his mid-twenties, he had expanded his operation to cattle and had leased large tracts of grazing land in Illinois. Before the age of thirty, Millikin was known as "the first cattle baron of the Prairie State."

In 1856 he settled in Decatur with $75,000, a sizable fortune for the time. Soon afterward Millikin wedded Anna Aston, to whom he remained married until his death in 1909. He purchased land between Pine Street and Oakland Avenue in Decatur and built one of the finest mansions the small town. In 1860, at the suggestion of business associates, Millikin went into the banking profession. His talent for business served him well, and the bank prospered. In 1896, the business had grown to the point that it built a seven-story office building with 125 rooms that was called by one critic, "the most pretentious office building in downstate Illinois."

Through the succeeding years, Millikin was also active politically and philanthropically. He was a close friend and supporter of Abraham Lincoln and served as a Macon County Supervisor for several years. However, it was for his generosity to his community that Millikin would be chiefly remembered. By the time of his death in 1909, Millikin had given away more than five hundred thousand dollars to charitable causes, primarily in the Decatur community.

Of the many generous gifts that Millikin left to his beloved Decatur, his university was his crowning achievement. In 1868, James Millikin purchased sixteen acres of wooded land just west of the downtown section. He leased the land to two local businessmen, who titled the area "Fairview Park" and used it as a site for local fairs, horse races, and community gatherings. Then in 1900 he reclaimed the park to begin his long-held dream of building a university. Plans were carefully developed, and in 1901 he received a charter from the state of Illinois for what was initially called the Decatur College and Industrial School.

The first president of the college, Dr. Albert Reynolds, arrived in Decatur in 1902, and construction on the initial buildings began that year. By the late spring of 1903, four main buildings had been constructed, and the college was ready to be opened. On June 4, 1903, Millikin was dedicated by President Theodore Roosevelt. On September 15, the Millikin University opened its doors to students for the first time. Initially, James Millikin had expressed his hope that the school might reach an attendance of five hundred within a few years. Instead, on the first day of registration, 562 students matriculated as the school's first freshman class. Millikin's dream of building a university had come true at last.

Through the years the campus has grown and new buildings have been added. Most blend beautifully with the original modified Elizabethan architecture of the campus, with mottle brick exterior and terra cotta ornamentation. In its look and ambiance, the current campus has retained much of Millikin's original plans and dreams. And, if the ghostlore attached to this venerable institution is true, it has retained other aspects of its history as well—unquiet spirits that roam the campus buildings, and link the lives of the living with the past of Millikin University.

Notably, the first bits of ghostlore attached to the land on which Millikin University now stands began long before James Millikin or his university came to the area. According to Troy Taylor, the first settlers to what is now Decatur whispered tales about the woods that lay just to the west of the settlement. It was told that the land was an Indian burial ground, and that as the sun set over the forest, the vengeful spirits of the dead braves rose from their graves to wander the woodland. Settlers are said to have carefully avoided the region after nightfall. Taylor also relates other stories told of the region prior to the existence of Millikin University. However, the first ghost story attached directly to the college itself is a sad story of a man known to the university and community as Tommy the Watchman.

Tommy the Watchman

In the early days of the university, a railroad spur belonging to the Wabash Railroad ran along the east end of campus. Since electrical railroad crossings were as yet undreamed of in those days, the railroad provided a watchman to guard the point where Oakland Avenue crossed the tracks. It was his job to provide warning of an impending train and make sure students crossing the intersection on their way to and from the university made their way safely.

Tommy the Watchman, as he was called, soon became a well known and beloved fixture among the students and community. He was known as courteous and gregarious, always having a friendly greeting for those whose welfare he guarded. When not on duty, Tommy lived in a small watchman's shanty provided him by the side of the railway spur.

With the advent of electrical warning gates, Tommy found himself unemployed, but he continued to live in the watchman's shanty that had been his home for many years. At night, those passing by would see the one window of the shed illuminated by the yellow light of a lantern, and would hear, floating through the night, the gravelly voice of Tommy singing out railroad tunes and familiar hymns.

In the mid 1920s, it was noticed by several citizens that Tommy was missing. A committee of students and local citizens approached the watchman's shanty, and, upon entering, found Tommy dead on his cot. The elderly man had evidently died peacefully in his sleep some days prior. A collection was started for his burial, and Tommy was laid to rest in Greenwood Cemetery.

With the passing of Tommy the Watchman, Decatur lost one of its favorite local characters. However, Tommy's story does not end here. Several months later, students passing by the shanty late at night on their way to a school function reported seeing the cabin lit up from within by the yellow glow of lantern light. Shocked, several students went to investigate, but as they approached the light faded. Entering the cabin, they found it empty.

Soon other students and local citizens began seeing the strange light moving around the shanty late at night. Some even recounted hearing a low voice singing out hymns as in years past. Inevitably, when someone drew near to the cabin, the light mysteriously disappeared, the night grew quiet, and the building was always found empty.

In the early 1920s, the railroad tracks were torn up and the flagman's shanty demolished. Still, through the years, passers by the area have reported seeing a lantern light moving in the vicinity of where the watchman's shanty once stood, and in the folklore of Decatur, it is said that Tommy the Watchman still keeps his watch.

The Spirit of Taylor Theater

Many universities throughout our nation can boast of a theater ghost, and Millikin University is no exception. The building where Taylor Theater now resides was built in the early years of the school as an assembly hall and classroom facility. In time the hall was renovated and renamed Shilling Hall. The large auditorium that had once served as the site of college assemblies was converted for use as a theater and renamed Taylor Theater after the first president of the university, Albert Taylor.

The identity of the ghostly presence in the theater is unknown. Some stories suggest it is the spirit of an unnamed child who resides within the theater walls. It is said that the child is playful and innocuous, prone to simple pranks and games. This story has given rise to the odd tradition of actors laying three pieces of candy on the stage prior to a performance to ensure the ghost's benevolence. Tales are whispered of technical mishaps and botched performances levied against those who do not appease the specter in this manner.

While such a story may sound much like standard theater superstition, other stories told of the ghost are of a more uncanny, and at moments even malevolent nature. The sounds of light footsteps and laughter have been heard in the auditorium when no one but the listener was present. Stage hands often speak of tools vanishing from plain view when their backs are turned. Lights are said to have mysteriously turned themselves on after the theater has been vacated and locked.

One stage hand recently recounted leaving a prop room to retrieve some materials, only to return a few moments later to find the door shut and locked—from the inside. "I know that I left the door standing open when I left," he now recalls, "and even if I had shut it, there was no way that door could be locked except from the inside. We had to search for a key, and when we finally got the door open the place was empty. It was spooky, to say the least."

Still, some might say that most of the phenomena reported from the Taylor Theater are of the type that can be relegated to the category of coincidence and imagination. At the very least, they seem to be the benign occurrences standard in these types of stories. One might be hard pressed, however, to convince at least one young woman of the harmless nature of the apparition of Taylor Theater.

As related in *The Ghosts of Millikin University,* Troy Taylor relates being approached in the summer of 1995 by a Millikin alumni

Photo: Troy Taylor

Shilling Hall, home of the ghost of Taylor Theater on the Millikin University campus.

who told him that one night that several years ago she was participating in a play at Taylor Theater. "I didn't believe in any of that stuff," she told Taylor, "and laughed at one of my friends who had brought candy for the ghost before the show that night."

A few moments before the curtain was to open, the girl, in costume, began descending the stairs from the dressing room to the backstage area when she clearly felt two small hands grab hold of her ankles. "I distinctly felt someone's fingers and I immediately looked down . . . and there was no one there," she told Taylor.

As the hands tightened their grip on her, the frightened girl struggled to free herself, only to feel her feet being pulled out from beneath her. Before she could scream, she pitched forward down the stairs, striking her head in the process and blacking out for several minutes. Needless to say, she missed her performance that night, and from then on she steadfastly observed the ritual of placing three pieces of candy on the stage to appease whatever spirit inhabits Taylor Hall. From her perspective there are some superstitions that are best assumed true.

The Ghost of the Old Gymnasium

Another ghost said to roam, or in this case run, through a building on the Millikin campus is the phantom jogger of the Old Gymnasium. The building in question was first constructed in 1911. At the university's inception, it is said that both James Millikin and president Albert Taylor were reluctant to allow athletics on campus, under the belief that they might inhibit the academic endeavors of students. However, within a year of the school's opening, both had relented and intercollegiate sports began there in 1903. Millikin's basketball teams won four state championships in the school's early days, and football and intramural sports programs prospered.

In 1911 the university's first gymnasium was built to accommodate the sports programs at Millikin and to allow students a place for recreation and physical fitness. The gymnasium itself was a huge space, with a basketball court on the main level and an elevated running track circuiting the circumference of the gymnasium, as well as a small room on a lower level.

As years passed, Old Gym was eventually replaced by the Griswold Physical Education Center, and today the lower level of the building is relegated for use as a weight room and a dance studio. The main gymnasium is now the domain of the theater department, which uses the space to store stage scenery and old sets. An inspection of the space finds it cluttered with props, stage flats and a thick layer of dust. Significantly, the area that was once the elevated running track is completely blocked by a collection of furniture, unused lighting equipment and lumber used for set construction.

Yet it is said that something runs the track still, something that is not inhibited by the track being blocked. During Christmas break in 1994, according to Troy Taylor, a Millikin security guard unlocked the front door late one night in order to make his rounds in the Old Gym. Usually, holiday breaks are a relaxed time for security personnel, as the campus is generally deserted and little activity is left to supervise. On Christmas eve the guard unlocked the front door of the old gym in order to make sure everything was secure in the structure. Making his way into the facility, he found the building dark and silent, as expected.

Almost silent. As the officer stood in the lobby, he could distinctly make out the sound of running footsteps originating from the second floor elevated track. As he made his way up the stairs toward the second floor, he could plainly hear the sound of a runner circling the gymnasium on the raised pathway. The incredulous guard realized this was impossible, as the track was rendered impassable by theater sets, yet as he unlocked the upstairs door, the sound of running was clear and unmistakable.

Cautiously the guard hit the light switch, illuminating the area in harsh light. Abruptly the sound ceased, and as the guard soon discovered, the running track area was empty. Understandably, the guard did not tarry in the precincts of the Old Gymnasium that night, but, quickly checking the rest of the building, made his exit.

This would not be the only appearance of a spectral presence in the old gymnasium. In his book Taylor also relates a story told to him by a woman who had once served as a costume designer for the theater department. The woman told Taylor of an experience she had late one night in the Old Gymnasium while working on costumes for an upcoming production. As the hour was late, the woman had taken care to ensure that the doors to the building were locked, and that she was alone in the facility.

She was startled, to say the least, then, when she heard the sound of a girl's crying floating to her ears from a downstairs section of the building. The mournful sound rose and fell, shattering the peace of the night with its melancholy reverberation. As the woman told Mr. Taylor, "It sounded as if her heart was broken."

Summoning all her courage, the woman walked to the stairwell and started making her way to the lower level. The crying grew louder and more dramatic, until, as she neared the bottom of the stairs, it turned into a warbling scream. However, the moment the costume designer placed her foot on the landing, the sound abruptly stopped, as though cut off by some unseen agency. A thorough search of the premises revealed that, as the woman had believed, she was alone, and the doors were securely locked around her.

Other incidents surrounding the Old Gymnasium abound. A number of years ago two students who were working late on a set design in the Old Gym, decided to leave for a few moments to get something to drink. When they returned less than an hour later, they found all of their tools missing from where they had left them when they had vacated the premises. A search of the building revealed no clue to the mystery, but when they returned the next morning, the tools had been replaced in their original location, despite the fact that the building had been empty and locked in the interim.

The Ghost of Gorin Library

Gorin Library opened its doors to the campus community in 1931. In architecture, it was designed to closely resemble many of the earlier building on campus, with a brick facade and an Elizabethan style. Since the addition of a new library facility to the campus a number of years ago, Gorin Hall has been used primarily to house administrative offices, including admissions and financial aid.

Nearly all of the stories associated with Gorin Hall revolve around a small room in the basement of the facility where, it is said, a maintenance worker died a number of years ago. Strange smells are known to permeate this room without explanation, and odd sounds have been heard coming from the area late at night. One staff member, locking the building late on an October afternoon not long ago, reported hearing the sound of a muffled hammering coming from the room. "I knew I should go down there and check it out," the staff member muses, "but I knew I was the last one in the building. Also, I had heard enough stores about that particular room that I could not get excited about going down there alone. I locked the door and drove home as quickly as I could."

Perhaps the most common phenomena reported by staff who visit the room is the uncomfortable feeling that they simply are not alone. One office staff member told Troy Taylor that he frequently became uncomfortable in the room. So strong were his feelings that he eventually resolved that he would no longer work in the room alone under any circumstances. A few days after reaching his decision, the young man abashedly confided his feelings to a co-worker. Instead of ridiculing him, however, the individual smiled broadly and said, "So, you've met our ghost, huh?" Indeed he had, as have many others over the years.

Spirits in the Women's Dormitories

On a college campus, dormitories are a place of life. Such residences are customarily filled with the sounds of students coming and going, studying and playing, and the genial hectic activity of young adults. Many of the complexities of college life are lived out within the walls of a dormitory. Yet, in some odd cases, dormitories may also be a place of death as well.

Many ghost stories found on college campuses find their origins in the tragic tales of murder and untimely death. Such are the cases of two tales found on the Millikin campus. These are two strange, sorrowful stories that, some believe, have led to even stranger consequences in a pair of women's residence halls.

The first such story is that of a disembodied spirit named Bonnie, who is said to dwell in Blackburn Hall on the Millikin campus. The spirit is that of a young coed who was brutally murdered in the building in the early 1960s. While the historical veracity of the tale may be open to question (no official record of such an event being available), according to the tales the woman was slain outside her dorm room late one evening and the killer never found. Although her exact name has never been ascertained, residents of Blackburn have christened her Bonnie in honor of Professor Bonnie Blackburn, after whom the building was named.

Whoever she might be, the ghost of Blackburn has made her presence known at the dormitory in a number of ways over the years. She has been see as a wispy figure encountered in the hallways, and has been credited with rooms suddenly turning cold for no apparent reason. Bonnie has also been known to play havoc with appliances in the hall, primary on the third floor, which seems to be her favorite haunt. Radios and televisions have been known to turn themselves off and on, seemingly of their own volition. On at least one occasion, a resident complained to Troy Taylor that Bonnie refused to allow her to listen to her stereo one night while studying. Every time she would turn on the music, she recalled, the switch would abruptly turn itself off. After several fruitless attempts to keep the stereo on, she finally simply gave up and studied in silence, allowing Bonnie her peace and quiet.

Meanwhile, two buildings south of Blackburn, another unruly apparition is said to haunt Aston Hall, the oldest woman's dormitory at Millikin. Built in 1907, the building is named for Anna Aston Millikin, wife of founder James Millikin. At the time of its completion, the dormitory was one of the most impressive buildings on campus. Five stories high, it accommodated a spacious dining room and kitchen, dean's office, and forty student rooms. Today, the building remains much the same as it did at the time of its construction, despite the encroachment of other buildings around it. Aston has retained its aura of genteel elegance throughout its long history. Further, some say that it has retained its resident ghost as well.

According to the legend of Aston Hall, the resident spirit is that of a former resident who committed suicide in the dormitory during the 1940s. Like her counterpart in Blackburn Hall, she is sometimes glimpsed as a shadowy figure seen in odd corners of the building late at night. Yet at moments she has been seen in a more solid form as well. At least once, the ghost was reported in one of the common bathrooms in the dormitory by a coed who at first noted only a strange girl in outdated clothing standing by one of the sinks. As the resident stared at the figure, she was stunned to note that although the figure seemed real, it ended just below the waist. As the girl stood, trans-fixed, the figure turned, smiled, and then seemed to evaporate into thin air.

More striking still are the stories of the feminine apparition stroll-ing the length of one dormitory wing. What makes this feat unique is the fact that the figure does not utilize the hallway for her promenade, but makes her way through the walls of the dorm rooms. She is said to appear out of one wall in a dorm room, float directly to the opposite wall, and then to pass through the wall into the next room, thus mak-ing her way down the length of the wing.

While on more than one occasion this performance has caused general alarm and consternation among the residents of Aston Hall, by and large the ghost is simply accepted as a part of the institution. As one student put it, "If the stories are true, then she is just one of us. Maybe she is here to check on our welfare. Everyone at Aston knows the stories, and we sort of like having her around."

Specters of Millikin's Greek System

The Greek system is yet another great source of campus ghostlore. Several at Millikin were recorded in the aforementioned book, *The Ghosts of Millikin University.* The haunting of the Sigma Alpha Epsi-lon (SAE) house is a classic among them.

In his book, Troy Taylor tells the story of a resident of the SAE house who related to him that one day he was sitting with his girl-friend on a couch in his second-floor room. On the opposite wall from where the couple sat was a dresser, on top of which sat two glass bottles. As the couple sat talking, they both noticed first one and then both of the bottles slowly rise from the dresser and float to the floor, landing so gently that they remained upright. No rational source for the movement could be found.

Taylor's informant, a young man named Jeff, also related several other incidents that have occurred in the fraternity. In the wee hours of one dark morning, residents of the house were rudely awakened by the sound of music suddenly blaring from one of the rooms normally inhabited by one of the brothers. Somewhat disgruntled by the fact that one of their members would be playing music so late at night, several members loudly pounded on the door of the room, demanding that the music be shut off immediately.

Their queries were met with silence, as the room was devoid of human inhabitants. Eventually one of the room's earthly residents was located across campus, and he immediately returned to the SAE house to unlock his door. When he and the other fraternity members entered the room, they found both the stereo system and the CD player turned on, and a compact disc playing. Unable to account for how this might have occurred, the member turned off the power to the stereo system. Only a moment later, the power went back on for both the receiver and CD player, and the CD began playing at the exact point it had been playing a moment earlier. Startled, the member reached out and pulled the plug from the wall, and this time, mercifully, the stereo remained silent. It should be noted that the stereo had displayed no such bizarre behavior before or since that night.

Another resident of the house reported an even more dramatic occurrence. He told Troy Taylor that he was sitting in his room studying one afternoon when he became cognizant of a strange noise emanating from his closet. He opened the door to be confronted with the sight of all his clothes, one after another, being torn from their hangers and dumped unceremoniously on the floor of the closet.

It was Taylor's informant Jeff who reported one of the sightings of the ghost. Several summers ago he related that he was staying at the fraternity over the summer break, when no one else was in the building. One night as he was dropping off to sleep in a third floor bedroom, he was awakened by a loud noise coming from the downstairs section of the house. Struggling to his feet, Jeff made his way downstairs to the new section of the house.

As he entered one of the common rooms, he was confronted with the sight of the hazy figure of a young man standing near the fireplace on the opposite side of the room. Though he could see the figure clearly, he realized that he could see through the young man's body, and that the figure faded away before it reached the floor. Surprisingly, the ghost turned toward him and did not seem menacing or frightening. According to Taylor, Jeff described the young man as being "human in appearance, but definitely not human." At first considering the possibility that he was still dreaming, Jeff paused to rub his eyes for a moment, but when he looked back the figure was still in the room. In a matter of a moment, however, the figure faded from sight.

Another fraternity at Millikin, the Kappa Sigma House, is said to be haunted by a ghost named Nathan, who, according to legend, is the shade of a former resident who hung himself in a bathroom in the upper floor of the house, called "the watchtower" by fraternity members. Since that time the bathroom has been renovated into sleeping rooms. A fraternity brother named Pat reported to Troy Taylor that he saw a spectral figure in the doorway of the recreational room on the first floor. He recalled:

> It looked like a half of a person sticking out from the corner of the wall. It seemed to be two dimensional and black. You could see through it but there was no definition or features to it at all. It literally looked like a shadow that was standing by itself.

Pat then called a friend from another room who came and saw the shape as well. The two then left the room to circle around through a passageway in order to come up behind the form, but when they did, it was gone.

Pat also related another story that took place in a room that was at the time reserved for the president of the fraternity. He and a friend were there one day talking when suddenly his friend was interrupted in midsentence by a loud voice in the room demanding "What are you doing here?" The two looked around the room, but naturally there was no one in the vicinity. As he related to Taylor, "We were alone in the house at the time. It was being renovated and we had the only keys." Pat then ran to university security office and brought back a guard, who searched the facility top to bottom, only to find it empty.

Other residents of the fraternity have reported the by-now-familiar phenomena of lights turning themselves off and on. Radios and at least once a set of stereo speakers have been known to launch themselves across the room for no explainable reason.

Another eerie manifestation occurred in a member's room that had a phone answering machine. The machine in question seemed to regularly start recording for no apparent reason. Perplexed, its owner disconnected the device from the incoming phone line, but the odd behavior continued. Odder still was the fact that on at least once occasion, when the tape was played back, a mysterious voice could be heard on the tape that did not belong to anyone in the fraternity.

The room where Nathan reportedly killed himself has been the site of other disturbances. Residents of the room once observed an alarm clock sitting on a dresser rise up into the air to a height where the cord attaching it to the electric outlet was pulled taut and then out of the wall.

A final unearthly story was reported by an fraternity alumni who came one summer to do some carpentry work on the second floor with a friend. As they worked with an electric saw, cutting some wood, naturally the sawdust filled the air. What was unnatural about it was that as it did so, both men clearly observed the outline of a figure in the dust. The alumnus immediately shut off the saw, the dust settled to the floor, and the figure was gone.

Not only the fraternities at Millikin can claim unearthly residents. At least one sorority, the Delta House, is the reported residence of a female apparition. The sorority, located on Park Place just west of campus, is a strikingly beautiful structure, with a carefully manicured lawn leading up to a white front porch with tall columns.

The revenant who is said to inhabit the house has often been encountered in a variety of forms by the women residents of the sorority. Strange whispers are heard in the upstairs dormitory, and footsteps echo in empty hallways. Most often, the ghost has been encountered in an upstairs dormitory section. According to *The Ghosts of Millikin University,* she is seen as the semitransparent figure of a woman with a faded dress. Her clothing seems to be in the style of early settlers in the area.

According to the stories told, this ghost has been seen by literally dozens of residents to the sorority. At least one resident alone claims to have seen the ghost a total of six times. She is sometimes spotted in the bedrooms of the house, but most often at the junction between the old and new sections of the dormitory section.

Some residents say they have awakened at night to see her standing over their beds. One such story was told by a girl who claimed that one night she was roused from sleep in the early hours of the morning to see a pale, ghostly face only inches away from her, staring down intently. One might only guess as to the hapless girl's reaction.

To talk with students and faculty at the institution, or to read Troy Taylor's *Ghosts of Millikin University,* one gets the impression that throughout the length and breadth of the Millikin campus, supernatural events are commonplace. In dormitories, fraternity and sorority houses, and even in some of the academic buildings, it is said that apparitions walk and specters peer from dark corners.

There are, it seems, some universities and colleges that do not harbor a campus ghost in their traditions. If so, then they must be the poorer for this deficit. However, Millikin University gratefully cannot be counted in this number. For, it seems that on this sedate Midwestern college, ghosts are nearly as plentiful as students willing to believe in them. Ultimately, the last word on this fascinating collection belongs to Troy Taylor, who writes:

> What of the of the ghosts of Millikin? Are they real, or the figments of some college student's imagination? I believe them to be real, and that there is something at Millikin University that defies explanation. What is it? I have no idea, and thus the search continues.

9
The Troubled Spirits of Marquette University
Marquette University
Milwaukee, Wisconsin

When traveling by the graveyard, late last night, Billy'n I had a terrible fright.
For there were the dead, parading proud, with brackish grin and moldy shroud.
Old English Folk Song

Picture the stereotypical college campus and one immediately conjures up the image of a quaint, colloquial setting among tall trees with ivy clinging to granite walls. A tour through many of the institutions of higher education throughout our nation provides many such examples. However, to limit ourselves to such a view is to belie the fact that many colleges and universities are set in much more metropolitan setting. Visit any major city in America and one will find, situated amidst the hustle and bustle of urban life, many of our nation's outstanding academic institutions.

One such example of a metropolitan campus is Marquette University in Milwaukee, Wisconsin. Resting squarely within the central commercial district of Milwaukee, the campus little resembles the classic image of a quiet, secluded academic setting. Chartered in 1864 as one of America's first Jesuit colleges, Marquette today is a thriving institution with a reputation for academic excellence. Overall, Marquette, by its own design, provides an education that is, according to a university publication, "strongly academic, Catholic and urban in nature."

Although Marquette University today stands in an urban setting surrounded by the trappings of modern life, tales are whispered from class to class, generation to generation, of spectral revenants that roam its corridors, keeping the past very much alive. Not one but several campus buildings are said to be inhabited by spirits of the undead.

One particular tale centers around the melancholy apparition of a young priest who is said to walk the halls of Johnson Hall. Serving today as a dormitory facility, Johnson Hall was first constructed to contain a large number of classrooms, laboratories, and a gymnasium. A portion of the fifth floor served as housing for Jesuit priests, many of whom had come to teach at the university.

In the early 1960s, one such priest came to live and teach at Marquette. A young man only recently ordained, the cleric had come to the university to teach mathematics. While such a post, so early in his career, was considered a mark of favor and distinction, still the young priest did not seem happy in his new position. Although not much is known about the clergyman in question, it is speculated that, like many men new to the priesthood, he struggled with his calling and the rigid demands placed upon him by his chosen vocation. Other reports hint that, while known to be brilliant in his field, his temperament made him uncomfortable and ill-suited to teaching in a university setting.

Whatever the cause, as time wore on the young priest grew more and more unhappy at Marquette. Although fulfilling his teaching duties, he became sullen and withdrawn. So deep was his melancholy that one of his superiors is said to have recommended that he be relieved of his duties in order to obtain psychological counseling. Before this suggestion could be acted upon, however, the unthinkable happened. On August 3, 1963, just before classes were to resume for the fall semester, the body of the young priest was found crumpled on the sidewalk immediately in front of Johnson Hall. Driven to insanity by the depth of his depression, he had jumped to his death from the fifth floor of the building.

Immediately the entire campus community went into mourning for the young man. Many in the campus and Jesuit communities at Marquette wondered aloud what had driven him to take his own life. This feeling of helpless grief was only deepened by the fact that, since suicide was considered a mortal sin in Catholic tradition, the priest could not be buried with the full rites and ceremonies that would normally have been afforded him. Instead, his body was quietly interred at a local cemetery, and life returned to normal at Johnson Hall.

Some wonder if life has ever returned to normal at Johnson Hall. Perhaps the unceremonious nature of the priest's burial, without the blessing of his church, left him with unsettled business. Perhaps whatever it was in life that so tortured his existence and drove him to untimely death also forced him to remain. Perhaps the priest returned to seek the peace that so eluded him in life. Whatever the cause, it is said that since the day of his sad death, his spirit has remained.

Most of the ghostly manifestations at Johnson Hall seem to be centered around the fourth floor where the unlucky priest stayed during his final days. Since the building has now been renovated into a dormitory, students reside where once priests lived and worked.

"Sometimes, when I am working alone at night, I feel an uneasiness in the building," then junior Angie Van De Hey told the campus newspaper, the *Marquette Tribune,* in 1996. "Sounds usually turn out to be janitors but you have to wonder."

Others, too, have reported strange sensations while in the pre-

Photo: Dan Johnson

Johnston Hall at Marquette University, which is said to be haunted by the ghost of a priest who committed suicide by jumping from a fifth story window.

cincts of the fourth floor of Johnson Hall. At least one security guard who routinely visits the area late at night to check on residents has reported the "odd sensation of not being alone" while on rounds there. Once, while checking the floor during Christmas break when the hall was empty, the guard reported feeling a sudden cold spot in the hallway.

"It was not a draft," he now says. "It was like a small area of intense cold—it made all the hair on my hands and on the back of my neck stand up," the guard recalls. This was accompanied by the feeling of a presence with him in the hallway. "I checked all the doors to make sure they were locked and then exited the floor quickly, I can assure you."

As word of the strange presence at Johnson Hall spread through the campus and surrounding community, interest in the haunting has risen. At least one amateur ghost hunter has volunteered his services at investigating the haunt. Jeffery Seelman, a native of the area, visited the hall on one occasion and came away believing there may be more than the spirit of the hapless mathematics professor residing there. Seelman was quoted in the *Marquette Tribune* as believing that the spirits of Native Americans might also haunt the building.

Having felt "negative spiritual energy" in the building, Seelman suspected that, considering Johnson Hall's proximity to the Menomonee River, it might have been built on an Indian burial ground. It is known that Native Americans who had lived on the land long before the university was established, routinely buried their dead near bodies of water. "When the church built the school, it didn't take into account the Indian energy in the ground. The founding fathers had good intentions, but no rituals were performed to appease the spirits," Sellman told the paper. "Whenever people mess with burial grounds, there are going to be angry spirits."

However precarious some might find Mr. Sellman's hypothesis, many at Marquette firmly believe in the presence of some strange presence haunting Johnson Hall. However, such stories are by no means unique to this building. Other campus buildings also have been reported to be haunted.

Residents have speculated that Tower Hall, also a dormitory, is haunted by a spectral presence which is said to reside on the seventeenth floor. The origins of such a story may hearken back to the colorful past of the building. In the early part of this century, Tower Hall was built as one of the grandest hotels in Milwaukee. During the 1920s and 1930s it received a host of notable visitors and guests. According to legend, Al Capone was a guest at the hotel at least once.

Perhaps Capone's legendary presence may be explained by the fact that the hotel apparently operated a "secret floor" featuring gaming and alcohol during Prohibition. From this "secret" seventeenth floor, the sounds of laughter and raucous celebrating were frequently heard during the second decade of our century.

One wonders if the party ever really ended. While the hotel in question closed long ago, through the years residents Tower Hall have reported the sound of laughter and merrymaking echoing through the empty halls of the seventeenth floor, which now is used to store machinery. According to local campus legend, residents of the sixteenth floor at Tower Hall have frequently been disturbed by eerie sounds from the seventeenth floor while studying late at night.

One person who tells the story is former student Daniel Nadolski*, who lived on the sixteenth floor of Tower Hall in 1980. Nadolski recalls lying awake in his bed at night and listening to the sounds of a party coming from the floor above him. Nadolski states that he could clearly hear the clink of glasses, snippets of conversation, and the sounds of dancing floating to his ears from the floor above. Stranger still was the fact that the sounds were accompanied by the eerie resonance of a piano playing ragtime music in the background.

Inevitably, when security officers arrive to investigate such disturbances, they find the seventeenth floor dark and vacant of any human habitation. However, somewhere in the midst of the dust and storage boxes of the infamous seventeenth floor, some remnant of the past might remain at Tower Hall.

Meanwhile, across campus, another hall is said to bear the spectral mark of its past. Humphry Hall, yet another dormitory on the Marquette campus, is the site of a macabre yet playful apparition. Before its acquisition by the university, Humphry Hall served as the Children's Hospital of Wisconsin. Though the last small patients were transferred from the building years ago and the sterile white ward-rooms transformed into dormitory suites, some odd presence is said to inhabit the building still.

Stories of Humphry Hall's haunting have circulated almost from the time of its acquisition by Marquette. One of the most recurrent problems deals with the dormitory elevator. Like many of its breed located in older buildings throughout our nation, this elevator is a bit cantankerous and has even been accused of "having a mind of its own." However, this particular elevator has, on occasion, evidenced behavior that suggest another influence was being exerted on it as well.

On at least one occasion, a student entering the elevator on the main floor pressed the third floor button in order to visit a friend, only to have the elevator instead descend to the basement, where the doors stood open for some moments. While such a malfunction might be written off as commonplace, what made this incident memorable was that, as the student waited for the doors to close, he was startled to hear ghostly footsteps approaching the elevator. A moment later, the doors closed and the elevator returned to the main floor.

Photo: Marquette University

Humphry Hall at Marquette University, formerly a children's hospital. The ghosts of its former patients are claimed to play in the hallways at night.

Other tales tell of the soft sound of children's laughter echoing down the dormitory hallways at odd hours of the day and night. One resident reported to the *Marquette Tribune,* "On one occasion I heard light knocking at my door. When I opened it, the hallway was empty but I heard what sounded like children's laughter coming down the hall.

According to the campus legend, one floor in particular, which formerly housed the intensive care ward for the Children's Hospital, has been particularly affected by the manifestations. One student who lived there in the mid 1960s reported feeling cold breezes in his room when all the windows were shut and no air conditioning was on. Stranger still was the time when the student, while in the shower, heard a dull thud from the cabinet next to the bathtub. Peering out of the shower, he was mystified to find that the door to the bathroom cabinet had come open and a container of baby powder had fallen from it, spilling its contents on the floor in front of the shower.

Turning off the shower, the young man carefully stepped over the spilled power and, wrapping a towel around him, went into the next room to find some means of cleaning up the mess. When he returned a few moments later, he was shocked to find several sets of small footprints had appeared in the powder. "I had not even heard of the ghost story before that," the student later told a friend, "but at that exact moment I became a believer."

Other students have also reported strange occurrences at Humphry Hall. Objects left in plain view in dormitory rooms have disappeared, only to later reappear in unlikely spots.

One student, at least, seems to have taken the phenomena in stride. Working late on Saturday night on a paper due the next Monday, he was disturbed several times by the sound of light scampering foot-steps in the hall outside his room and a sound like a ball being bounced along the corridor. Each time the young man rose to investigate, how-ever, he found the hallway deserted, with most other students either in bed or gone for the weekend. Finally, after being disturbed from his work several times, the young man flung open his door in despera-tion and called out into the darkness, "Whoever the hell you are, I wish you would cut it out. I am trying to get a degree here!" Perhaps the playful visitors understood, for he was disturbed no more that night.

Across the Marquette campus, such stories are told and retold. Like the mist that rises from the river on a spring morning, clinging to the ground till evaporated by the sun, so the tales told cling to the university, reminding us of its past. But more than that, perhaps they remind us that even in the most cosmopolitan of settings, spirits may still linger and the specters of the past may not be entirely gone.

10
The Guardian Spirit of Clet Hall
Niagara University
Lewiston, New York

So long as the stories multiply, and so few are positively explained away, it is bad method to ignore them.

William James

Many college campuses across our nation can boast of beautiful and even striking settings. From the rugged coast of Maine to the pastoral landscapes of the Midwest, many campuses offer unique and panoramic backdrops to the educational endeavors pursued there. No college, however, can claim more imposing surroundings than Niagara University located in Lewiston, New York. Set on the highest point of Monteagle Ridge, overlooking the Niagara gorge and nearby Niagara Falls, the university is situated amid breathtaking natural splendor.

The college was founded in 1856 as "Our Lady of Angels," a Roman Catholic institution attached to the Order of St. Vincent De Paul. Originally chartered both as an institution of higher education and a Roman Catholic Seminary, today the school no longer houses a seminary, but still maintains its strong ties to the Roman Catholic Church, as well as to the "Vincentian Order," as it is known.

The motto of the University, *Ut Omnia Te Cognito,* is borrowed from the Gospel of St. John and can be translated, "that all may know you." In the 142-year history of Niagara College, the gospel of Christ has been preached and taught to generations of students. Moreover, commitment to God has been lived out many times over the passing generations in the dedication of the countless priests who have devoted their lives to this vaunted institution.

Ironically, this very selfless devotion, exhibited by one heroic young priest, has given rise to the ghostly legend of the school. For it is said that within the walls of gothic Clet Hall, the gentle, benevolent spirit of a brave young clergyman lingers still.

An official campus tour package, distributed to visitors and prospective students, carries the short notation, "Thomas Hopkins, a student from Brooklyn, was killed in the fire of December 5, 1864. Legend has it that his ghost still haunts Clet Hall."

Such a terse notation, while interesting, does not begin to do service to the legend of Thomas Hopkins, the story of his life and untimely death and the ghost stories that have been attached to his name in the years that followed.

Not much can be ascertained about the background of seminarian Thomas Hopkins. It is known that he was born in Brooklyn, New York, in about 1840. It is conjectured that he may have been born to one of the large Irish immigrant families that came to America due to the great potato famine about that time. If indeed this is the case, then it may be surmised that his background was family oriented and devoutly Catholic. Perhaps this is why Thomas Hopkins came to Niagara University in 1862 to pursue his studies toward the priesthood.

Whatever his background, legend states that Thomas Hopkins was well suited both to his studies and his prospective vocation. According to the tales, Hopkins's years at Niagara were both happy and productive. In the classroom, Hopkins is said to have been bright and energetic, displaying a keen intellect and an affinity for religious study. Outside the classroom, he was known to be gregarious and well liked by both the older priests on campus and members of the student body.

When not involved in studies, Hopkins would frequently be found wondering the wilderness of the Niagara gorge. On warm afternoons he would often walk for hours, basking in the splendor and awesome beauty that surrounded him. According to the old stories, Hopkins loved his college, and found his life at the school to be fulfilling personally and academically. It was as though this amiable young man had found his place—a place, some whisper, that he has never left.

According to legend, so adept was Hopkins at his studies that in 1864, as he entered his third year of seminary, he was asked to serve as the "proper" at Clet Hall. In this capacity, he was to supervise the life of the students staying in the dorm, watch over the facility, and enforce university discipline where necessary. Although still young, Hopkins was considered to be an ideal choice for the position because of his maturity and amiable temperament.

Although not explicitly stated in his duties, Hopkins was also to be the unofficial guardian and caretaker for an elderly priest who lived on the top floor of Clet Hall. This old cleric, long since retired from active ministry, was housed in the upper floor attic area of the building and although still considered self sufficient, occasionally needed the additional care of a younger man.

Once again, Hopkins was found to be well suited to his duties. According to the tales told of him, his time at Clet Hall was satisfying for him as well as for all concerned. His innate affinity for people, together with his affable demeanor, made him a natural choice for dealing with the students who had been entrusted to his charge. Additionally, his caring ministrations to the elder priest residing there endeared him to the older man. Soon Hopkins found himself regarding the older gentleman as a second father and often the two would talk together well into the night. Hopkins found in the older man a font of wisdom and experience and the older cleric was delighted to have the comfort and companionship which Hopkins afforded him.

All might well have progressed along this pleasant and uneventful path had not tragedy struck. On the quiet afternoon of December 5, 1864, a fire erupted in the so-called "Philosopher's Room" on the third floor of Clet Hall.

According to a story published the next day in the *Lockport Journal and Courier:*

> The fire caught from a stove pipe which passed through the ceiling...The wing where the fire originated being of wood and very dry, the fire spread rapidly. The building was entirely destroyed.

The account of the inferno concluded with this note:

> One young man, a student named Hopkins, of Brooklyn, was too venturesome and, in his endeavor to save some of the property, was buried in the ruins.

Such was the official report of the blaze and the tragic death of Thomas Hopkins. However, accounts at the time suggested an even more poignant element to the story.

According to a long-told tale, on that fated afternoon Thomas Hopkins was returning to his beloved Clet Hall from one of his afternoon rambles along the Niagara gorge at about 2:30 when he was horrified by the sight of fire billowing from an upstairs window. Already students were pouring out of the dormitory and, after making sure that the fire department was on its way, Hopkins checked to make sure all of his charges had escaped the conflagration. A quick check revealed all safe, except one: the elderly priest of whom Hopkins had become so fond was nowhere to be found.

By this point, much of the building was engulfed in flames and it was obvious that to enter the fiery structure would be foolhardy if not suicidal. Still, without a second thought, Hopkins raced through the growing crowd of onlookers and, skirting past those who would constrain him, rushed headlong into the inferno. His actions, heroic and selfless, were nevertheless futile. A few moments after Hopkins entered the building, the structure, weakened by the fire, collapsed, burying both Hopkins and the elderly cleric he had sought to rescue.

While there is no sure historical record of the death of the elderly priest, it is known that on December 6, 1864, workers combing the wreckage of Clet Hall discovered the body of Thomas Hopkins buried beneath the charred rubble. His body was taken to a nearby morgue and then shipped to his native Brooklyn for burial. So passed a noble, brave young man whose dedication and love for others had cost him his life. However, some would argue that his story did not end with his internment.

In time, the shock and sadness of the event passed at Niagara University. Eventually winter turned to glorious spring, and as the world once more turned green and warm, the school administration began to make efforts to put the tragedy behind it. It was announced that Clet Hall would be rebuilt. While some structural modifications were made from the original plans for the building, when completed the new Clet Hall bore a striking resemblance to its predecessor. One added feature, however, was the addition of a stone obelisk before the main entrance of the building. Etched into its granite face was the simple inscription,

To the Memory of Thomas F. Hopkins

This memorial, dedicated to the memory of one so devoted to his university and its students, seemed reverently appropriate. However, if the stories that have been handed down for many generations at Niagara are true, this stone epitaph is not all that has been left behind as a reminder of Thomas Hopkins. Over the years, a great many stories have been told regarding the ghost of Clet Hall. So well known are the legends surrounding the building that it is considered a rite of passage for freshmen staying there to be initiated by hearing of the ghostly tales.

It is said that in the mid 1950s, one young student was sneaking back to his room after university curfew, returning from a late date in town. Quietly, he made his way to his second floor room, hoping to avoid notice by his resident assistant, one of the upperclassmen assigned to each floor to supervise the students living there.

As the freshman padded silently down the hall toward his room, he was startled to see a tall young man dressed entirely in black, standing in the hallway next to the door to his room. Thinking that perhaps he had been caught by a new resident assistant, the student approached the figure, no doubt groping for some valid excuse for his tardiness. When he was within a few feet of the figure, however, the tall man turned toward the student, smiled, and vanished. Shocked beyond words, the young man stood in the silent hallway alone for several minutes before daring to open the door and enter his room. The student in question is said to have been more careful to return before curfew from that point on.

In 1969, student John Matthews* lived for a semester in Clet Hall. One night he and a roommate were studying late in the evening when Matthews, fatigued by his mental labors, succumbed to his temptation to smoke a cigarette. Although it was against university policy to smoke in a dorm room, Matthews decided that this minor infraction of university rules would go undetected if he were to open the dorm window to allow the room to air out.

Going to his desk, he opened a drawer and retrieved an ashtray and pack of cigarettes. Lighting one, he crossed the room and opened the window. As Matthews turned back to his desk, the window was violently slammed shut as though by some unseen force.

As the shaken boy turned in the direction of his desk, he saw the ashtray he had left there a moment before levitate three inches from the surface of the desk, pause for an instant, and then soar six feet across the room, landing at the feet of his roommate. "It was at that moment that I decided to give up smoking, at least in my dorm room," Matthews now recalls with a smile.

Other stories abound. One dorm supervisor in the 1970s, alone in the building over spring break, is said to have chased the sound of running footsteps through the building one night, thinking that an intruder had entered. His chase ended when the footsteps ran up to a blank wall and then abruptly stopped. Subsequent investigation showed that the dorm was securely locked, and no intruder was on the premises.

New stories regarding encounters with the spirit of Clet Hall have appeared with regularity over the passing decades and continue to do so today. Marty Bourke, a graduate student at Niagara, has been the resident director of Clet Hall since the summer of 1996. However, even before taking that position, Bourke was well acquainted with the stories told of the spirit, having heard them as an undergraduate. Upon taking the job as resident director, Bourke was curious about the stories, and just what he might encounter in his position. He was soon to find out.

Bourke is careful to point out that the manifestations occurring in Clet are not of a malevolent nature. "They are more mischievous— nothing really harmful," he says. His indoctrination with the resident specter began in the summer of 1996, just a few weeks before students returned for the fall semester. Alone in the building, Burke rose early one morning and made his way to the large bathroom down the hall to shower. After a few moments in the shower, however, Bourke noted that the water pressure suddenly decreased drastically. Passing off the thought as a natural occurrence in an old building, Bourke finished his shower and stepped out to dry off. Then Bourke discovered the reason for the decreased water pressure. All of the showers and sinks in the bathroom had been turned on full force, greatly decreasing the water supply to his shower.

"I know for a fact that I was alone in the building," Bourke now says. "There was simply no way for someone to get in, let alone sneak in to the bathroom and turn on every faucet and shower there."

Soon Bourke was to hear of other baffling encounters with the spirit of Clet Hall. In the summer of 1997, when Bourke and a few resident assistants were living in the building, he was unceremoniously awakened by a 2:00 A.M. phone call from a distressed resident assistant. "He was really spooked," Bourke remembers today.

The young resident assistant, whose name was Jerry Sass*, reported to Bourke that he had been awakened from a deep sleep by the sound of someone running up and down the hallway in front of his third floor room.

Perplexed as to the origin of the sounds, Sass stuck his head out the door, ready to order someone to stop, but the hallway was empty. Now Sass was convinced that he was a victim of some sort of a bizarre joke. Clearly someone had run down the hall and quickly turned the corner next to his room in order to avoid detection. However, as he returned to his room and was in the process of closing the door, he heard the footsteps and laughter come from the other direction, rounding the corner and proceeding down the long hallway to the left of Sass's door.

Thinking now that he would get to the bottom of this hoax, Sass flung open the door and jumped into the hall, only to hear the footsteps abruptly stop and to find the hallway vacant. Bourke recounts, "That hallway is a long one with no way to avoid being seen. All the doors were locked and there is no way you could run that direction and not be caught." Perhaps the answer lies with the spirit of Clet Hall, enjoying one of his midnight rambles.

Interestingly, Bourke relates that the phenomena became more frequent in 1992, when the dorm went coed. "I kind of think when we went from a single sex dorm to coed, we sort of offended the sensibilities of either Thomas Hopkins or the older priest who died in the fire. They may not like both men and women living in the same dorm."

While such a conjecture is, of course, only speculation, it may well explain the experience of one young woman named Barbara Ann who lived in Clet one year shortly after the dorm went coed. Rising early to prepare for class one morning, the woman entered the communal bathroom to shower. After showering, she dressed and then went to the sink to brush her teeth. Bending close to the sink, the girl was stunned to see writing suddenly appear in the steam that covered the mirror over the sink before her. As she watched, horrified, first letters and then words began to appear literally inches from her face, as though traced with a human finger. Slowly the enigmatic message emerged:

It's not me.

While no one has yet offered an explanation as to the meaning of the message, its appearance caused a great deal of consternation among the students living at Clet Hall.

Other stories abound. Recently, one young man came to his resident assistant with an eerie story. He reported that one night during the first months of his stay at Clet Hall, he had been awakened from a sound sleep by the intense feeling of "a presence" in his room. So strong was this uneasy sensation that he could not return to sleep but instead lay awake, trying to rationalize the strange feeling away. As he did so, the young man happened to glance toward the opposite side of his room.

Suddenly his breath caught in his throat. There in the dim light he could see the figure of a man kneeling next to the room's couch, as in an attitude of prayer. Unable to believe his eyes, the student watched in terrified curiosity as the figure stayed in its position, immobile, for several moments and then seemed to melt into the dark air. Somewhat understandably, the young man was reluctant to report this unearthly appearance to his roommate, lest his friend think him delusional. However, several weeks after the event, the student in question gathered up enough courage to confide his experience to his roommate.

Instead of ridiculing the young man, however, his roommate stared wide-eyed as he described the apparition and then replied that he too had seen the figure not once but several times in recent weeks. In each case, the young men described their visitor as a man dressed in black kneeling next to their couch with his head bowed, as though in intense prayer or meditation.

As inexplicable as this visitation might seem to some, at Clet Hall it is common place. As with many haunted locales, the ghost of Clet Hall seems to have become a part of life there and accepted as a matter of course. Marty Bourke believes that he might even have discovered the domain of the ghost. Bourke relates the story that in the summer of 1997, he and several resident assistants living in the dorm decided to do some minor sprucing up in the building. As their first project, they decided to explore and clean the vast attic of the hall. Normally kept locked, this expanse had been shut up for decades.

As they crept through the cobwebs and thick dust, they discovered, positioned in front of a window overlooking the beautiful panorama of the Niagara gorge, a chair pulled up to face the window. Before it lay an open copy of a college yearbook from many years before. While this discovery might have seemed no more than curious, what added to the mystery was the fact that although a thick coat of dust covered nearly the entire attic and everything stored there, no dust was found on the chair or on the open book lying before it.

"It was like someone had recently been sitting on the chair looking out the window and looking at the yearbook," Bourke says. "It was like it was supposed to be set up that way. That spooked me a little bit. That was the only time I got a little spooky."

Interestingly, as Marty Bourke or anyone at Niagara speaks of the ghost of Clet Hall, there seems to be neither fear nor a sense of foreboding in their words. More than simply being an accepted part of life at Clet, many with connections to the hall have come to regard whatever spirit walks there as a benevolent presence.

Marty Bourke puts it best when he comments, "It is hard for me to believe in ghosts. So . . . I think of him more as an angel. Because, the way the story goes, Thomas Hopkins really enjoyed his time here at Niagara and since he gave his life trying to save someone else . . . maybe as a reward he was left to watch over us."

Perhaps, as Bourke believes, the spirit of Thomas Hopkins has been allowed to stay on at Clet Hall as some sort of divine reward for a selfless and devoted life that ended in a noble attempt to save another. Perhaps, as some suggest, he is joined in his reverie by the spirit of the elderly priest he so valiantly tried to save.

Whatever the case, on the campus of Niagara University, so picturesquely set amid the wonders of nature, it is considered a matter of fact that as darkness draws near and shadows grow long in Clet Hall, there walks the noble spirit of a selfless young man condemned, or perhaps blessed, to watch over those who live there—a kind, gentle spirit known as the ghost of Clet Hall.

11
The Ghosts of Kenyon College
Kenyon College
Gambier, Ohio

If a step should sound or a word be spoken,
Would a ghost not rise at the stranger's hand?

Algernon Charles Swinburne

Nestled in the rolling countryside of central Ohio, adjacent to the little town of Gambier, stands Kenyon College. A small liberal arts college, Kenyon was established in 1824 as a Christian institution attached to the Anglican Church and today serves a student population of fifteen hundred. Like many such colleges that dot the Midwest, Kenyon College is steeped in its own history and tradition. Many luminary leaders have come and gone through the portals of Kenyon College. Poets Robert Penn Warren and Jerry David Madden have linked their names to this great educational institution, as have several business, political and educational leaders.

One of the more unique aspects of this school is the myriad of ghostly tales that abound there. While many colleges can boast of a resident specter or two, the sheer volume of ghost stories associated with this small college and the pride the university invests in its unearthly inhabitants mark it as truly unique in the annals of college ghostlore.

According to an article in the *Kenyon Collegian,* a self proclaimed psychic appearing on the Phil Dohahue television program several years ago described Kenyon College as "the most spiritually active and evil place on earth." Though it might seem hard for any institution, particularly a small Midwestern college, to live up to that sort of epithet, in fact Kenyon staff and students willingly claim a whole legion of ghost stories as their credentials to the title. In fact, for many years the peculiar and somewhat bizarre rumor has circulated that Kenyon is located over the "gates to hell." While some colleges might disdain such a reputation as unfortunate, Kenyon seems to take an odd pride in the legend, although variants of the story place the gates to the abyss at different locations on campus.

From this strange beginning, the legends and supernatural stories attached to Kenyon College naturally unfold. Some are linked directly to tragic events from the college's history. Some ghost tales bear no apparent link to the past, and indeed no clear identity can be established for the apparitions in question. In the past several years, much has been written of the ghosts of Kenyon. The college archives department maintains a volume of records concerning these stories and articles about them have been featured in local and national publications. Chris Woodyard, the undisputed authority on of Ohio ghostlore, has written extensively regarding Kenyon College in her wonderful book, *Haunted Ohio.* While other universities may challenge the title of "America's Most Haunted College," it can be said definitively that no other college takes more pride in its specters than does Kenyon College.

One of the most famous ghost legends attached to the college involves Shaffer Dance Studio, a small performing arts building on campus. While today the studio is used for classes in the performing arts, the stories concerning the building take their origin in a time several years ago when the facility housed the university pool and a fatal accident is said to have occurred there.

The specifics of the tale vary from telling to telling. In some variants, a diver jumping from the three-meter board hit his head on the way down and sustained fatal head injuries. Other variants state the student was actually diving from the ten-foot board and that he bounced higher than expected, cracking his head against the glass ceiling over the pool and breaking his neck. An alternate story suggests that it was not a student who died at all, but a member of an Air Force unit stationed at the college during World War II for training in meteorology.

Whatever the case, stories of the phantom of Shaffer have been recorded on campus for years. Ghostly footsteps are said to have been frequently heard in and around the pool section, and students say they hear splashing sounds coming from the pool when no human inhabitants were in the area. Members of the swim team, who have come to look on the ghost with a sort of fondness, still report vague feelings of unease in the pool, particularly when there alone.

Other tales were even more specific. In 1971, the Kenyon swim team conducted a weekend long "swim marathon" to raise money for charity. As a precaution, it was arraigned for there to be at least two people in the pool at all times—a swimmer and a "spotter" whose job was to count the laps swam and ensure the safety of the swimmer.

At one point late during the first evening of the marathon, the spotter, seated in a chair overlooking the pool, became aware of an intense feeling of a "presence" in the pool area. Unable to shake off the eerie feeling, the young man focused his attention on counting the laps being swam, yet again and again the feeling that he was being watched disturbed him. Finally, as he sat silently watching the swimmer in the pool before him, the spotter heard what he later described as a cheery voice calling out his name from the locker room. Thinking that another member of the swim club had entered the building and was preparing to come into the pool area, the spotter excused himself from his appointed duties and walked into the locker room. It was empty, as was the entire building.

On another occasion several years later, a very similar incident occurred. Again, during a swim club "swimathon," a student sat early one morning watching a fellow team member laboriously swimming laps before him. Like the spotter several years before, as the hours wore on this young man also became are of the strange feeling of someone or something else present in the pool area. However, instead of trying to dismiss the feeling, the young man decided to call in reinforcements. Going to a public phone by the poolside, he dialed the number of a friend. Rousing the young man from sleep, he asked him if he would be willing to come down and join him poolside. Curious and somewhat disgruntled by this late night call, the friend inquired as to the reason for the sudden invitation. As the student at the pool attempted to explain his feelings, realizing how foolish they sounded, suddenly he was interrupted by a voice over his shoulder cheerfully calling out, "hi!"

So startled was the student that he dropped the phone and spun around. However, when he did so, there was no one in the area. From his vantage point at the phone, with a clear view of the pool and surrounding area, he saw that he was alone, save for the lone swimmer making his way to and fro in the pool. Thinking that his imagination was getting the best of him, the student picked up the phone and was about to explain the situation to his friend, but before he could do so the friend asked, "Who was that who said hello just a minute ago? Aren't you alone down there?" A good question indeed.

A similar question must have rushed through the mind of student Steve Killpack, who served as lifeguard for the Shaffer pool in 1979. According to an article in the *Kenyon Alumni Bulletin,* one night that spring, after ensuring that the last of the swimmers had departed Shaffer Hall, Killpack carefully extinguished the lights in the building, locked the building and took his leave. However, as he climbed the hill behind Shaffer Hall, making his way back to his dormitory, Killpack happened to glance over his shoulder at the hall and suddenly froze in his tracks. The lights in the pool area were on once again. Moreover, even from his position on the hill, Killpack could clearly hear the sound of loud splashing coming from the pool area. Unsure of just what to make of the strange turn of events, Killpack returned to Shaffer Hall and unlocked the front entrance. As he entered the pool area, the sound of splashing abruptly stopped, and although the lights in the pool area were indeed on, there was no one in the building.

Undaunted by his first encounter with the spirit, on another occasion Killpack led a group of his friends on a late night tour of the facility. As they entered the basement section and neared the boiler room, the door to the room, which was customarily locked, flew open before them. The room was empty, and the open door was examined and found in the locked position.

In 1984, Shaffer Pool was converted into Shaffer Dance Studio. However, according to the stories told of the premises, this has not deterred the resident ghost from its preternatural escapades. One campus story relates that shortly after the opening of the dance studio, a senior student was alone one night in the hall, practicing for an upcoming recital. As she moved through her dance, carefully concentrating on her choreography, she was bewildered to hear the sound of a diving board being stepped upon, followed by the sound of water splashing. Not once but several times the sound came, ringing out through the empty recesses of the building.

Investigating, she became convinced that the sounds were emanating from the women's locker room. As she approached the door to investigate, her curiosity turned to fear as she noticed wet footprints leading from the hallway into the locker room. Summoning all her courage, she opened the door and entered the locker room, only to find it dark and empty. Moreover, as she looked back to trace the path of the wet footprints, she discovered that they went directly from the doorway to a concrete wall and then stopped, as though whatever entity had made them had gone up to and then *through* the wall.

Other odd incidents are said to occur in the studio with some regularity. According to Chris Woodyard in *Haunted Ohio,* showers in the locker room are said to turn themselves on and off without human aid. Similarly, radios left unplugged at poolside have been found mysteriously reconnected with the volume turned up when no one has been in the vicinity. Further, it is popularly accepted on campus that those passing by the dance studio late at night have been known to see the lights mysteriously lit and the sounds of splashing coming from the confines of the hall. A few have even stated that as they hurried from the area, they have glanced over their shoulder to see a face staring at them from a small window overlooking the former pool area.

In fact, with the passing of time, the so-called "pool ghost" has garnered much attention on campus and even across the nation. The resident spook of Shaffer Hall has been written up in several regional and national magazines, including an article in *Sports Illustrated.* Interestingly, this phantom has become known almost affectionately on campus, particularly by the vaunted Kenyon swim team, who consider the ghost a good luck mascot.

In fact, many of the ghosts on campus are seen as simply a part of the campus community. Perhaps this is why the spirits are so numerous here. Not one but two freshman dormitories are said to have unofficial spectral residents. Norton Hall is said to be inhabited by the spirit of a girl who lived there many years ago. According to the old tale, the girl was afflicted with insomnia and spent many nights restlessly pacing the halls, waiting in vain for sleep to come. Finally, whether because of her affliction or because of some other distressing factor, the girl ended her life. Since her tragic self-destruction, footsteps have been reported traipsing the halls of Norton in the still of night. More than a few young women have reported hearing footsteps passing their door late at night and upon investigation, found the hallway empty.

Meanwhile, at Lewis Hall, legend states that a mischievous spirit is known to play practical jokes on students living there. Like his cohort at Norton Hall, he is said to be the shade of a suicide victim. According to campus legend (unsubstantiated by historical records) the Lewis Hall ghost is that of a young man who hung himself in an attic room long years ago. Though the room has since been vacated and the entrance boarded over, the apparition of the ill-fated student continues to haunt the hall.

In a paper submitted for a college history class, student Heather Frost relates some of the antics of this roguish spirit. Frequently passersby on campus near the hall have reported seeing a light burning in the attic room once inhabited by the student, despite the fact that power to the attic was shut off years ago. Further, the ghost does not confine himself to the scene of his demise and is said to roam the halls looking for victims for his pranks.

Frost relates that in 1987, strange events began to occur in the second floor room of student Eric Chambers. The manifestations began unobtrusively enough. That fall Chambers noticed his stereo system had begun to exhibit an odd malfunction. The radio was seen to visibly turn itself on for a few seconds and then turn itself off. This happened on several occasions when more than one witness was present.

This was just the beginning. Chambers says that one evening as he was sitting in his room with a number of friends, their reverie was disturbed by a knock at the door. Chambers called for the visitor to enter but no one responded. Someone got up and opened the door but the hallway outside was empty. This odd occurrence repeated itself several times in succession until, convinced that they were the victims of a joke, Chambers and his friends set a trap for the prankster. One student stood just inside the door, ready to open it at the first indication of a knock. When the loud rap came, the student sprang forward and opened the door suddenly. Though only a split second had elapsed since the rap on the door, the hallway was vacant. As Heather Frost's paper concludes, the occupants of the room that night were left with only one surmise—the ghost of Lewis Hall had struck again.

Other odd occurrences have been reported in Lewis over the years. Showers are said to turn themselves off and on. Similarly, appliances in the dorm rooms seem to have minds of their own, activating and then deactivating themselves at will. It is even said that on occasion all the toilets in one large bathroom have been known to flush themselves at the same moment despite the fact that no one is in their proximity. The ghost of Lewis Hall has a macabre sense of humor.

While the spirits said to inhabit the Lewis and Norton Halls are of a mischievous nature, an even more enigmatic ghost reportedly dwells in the athletic facility at Kenyon, Werthemer Hall. On several occasions, security officers, checking on Werthemer late at night, have related hearing the sound of someone running on the upstairs track. On each occasion when the officer investigated and turned on the bright overhead lights, the footsteps stopped and the track was vacant.

An even more startling event occurred several years ago to student Paul Schoenegge. According to an article in the *Kenyon Alumni News,* one night in 1975, Schoenegge, a trainer for the football team, returned with his coach to the fieldhouse after their opening game. The coach asked Schoenegge to take a film projector they had carried with them down to the basement where it was normally stored. The trainer readily agreed.

As he later recalled to the press, Schoenegge went down to the basement and put the projector down for a moment in order to use the restroom. Before he could get to the bathroom, however, he heard the sound of music coming from one of the storage areas in the basement. Assuming that a record player located there had somehow been left on, the student approached the storage cage, only to hear the music stop suddenly and find that the record player was unplugged and still.

Now perplexed, the student returned to pick up the film projector and approached the coach's office. Undoubtedly it was his intent to place the projector in its rightful place and then quickly vacate the premises, but perhaps whatever presence lingers in the area had other ideas. As Schoenegge approached the coach's office, the door, which would normally have been locked, sprung open to greet him, revealing a dark and apparently empty office.

With some trepidation, the young man moved forward into the office. Searching for a light switch, he tripped over something he later described as a human body and fell headlong. Jumping to his feet, the young man found the light switch immediately and turned to survey the room. It was utterly, inexplicably empty.

While such odd goings on would seem shocking at most college campuses, at Kenyon they seem commonplace. The college playhouse, Hill Theater, is also said to be haunted. Some members of the college campus believe the theater was built over the sight of a fatal car crash some years ago. While there is no historical record of such an event, drama students have developed the practice of leaving one light burning on stage constantly to appease the ghosts said to sojourn there. Heather Frost, in her unpublished paper, "Shades of Purple," writes that at least one security guard has reported constantly finding this light turned off while making his nightly rounds. The guard confided to Frost that in checking the building at night, he would often find the light unscrewed from its base. Carefully screwing the light back in, he would lock up the building and resume his rounds, only to come back several hours later to find it unscrewed again. The security officer also told Frost that often he would find the stage curtain closed on one of his nightly rounds, only to come back later and find it open, despite the fact that the building had been locked and vacant in the interim.

Another strange apparition is said to inhabit Room 13 of Leonard Hall. Although the room has been vacant and used for storage since the early 1960s, students in the dormitory have wondered if someone or something still occupies the room. In 1980 a student living next door to Room 13 reported hearing the sound of a bed squeaking in the room on numerous occasions. Subsequent investigation showed no bed in the room. Another student living on the floor reported showering early one morning and hearing the door to the bathroom open and the sound of someone entering. Peeking out from behind the shower curtain, she was shocked to see no one in the room.

What is perhaps most puzzling and even problematic about this haunting is the fact that, according to university records, no student has ever stayed in Room 13. However, this fact does little to dissuade the students living in Leonard from believing that the room is inhabited by something otherworldly.

Indeed, many of the stories related to the university cannot have their historical roots proven to any degree of certainty. However, three of the more infamous ghosts of Kenyon are tied to three distinct tragedies known to have occurred at the school.

One such tragedy, which has yet to be fully explained, involved the death of a young man in an elevator shaft at Caples Hall on November 8, 1979. Little is known about the accident itself. It seems that the young man in question had gone to a party that night on campus and then returned to Caples Hall, where he shared a room on the eighth floor with several roommates. Before going to his room, however, he apparently stopped briefly to visit his girlfriend on the sixth floor, staying a few moments before taking his leave. When last seen the young man was entering the elevator, apparently going back to his room on the eighth floor for the remainder of the night.

He never arrived. What happened in the confines of the elevator that early morning will never be precisely known. Later reports speculated that the elevator malfunctioned, stopping between the seventh and eighth floors. After prying the doors open, the young man might have seen an opening of about ten and one-half inches, leaving him barely enough room to slide out of the elevator and onto the floor below. Foolishly, he might have tried to do so.

If this is indeed the case, then somehow he missed. In any case, that night the young man met a tragic death, his body plummeting eight stories to the bottom of the elevator shaft.

At about 7:30 the next morning, a maintenance worker checking the building noted that the elevator was not functioning. A repairman was called, who found the elevator lodged between the seventh and eighth floors. Looking down the shaft, the repairman was horrified to see the crumpled form of the young man's body. Emergency medial personnel were called immediately and the young man was taken to a Mt. Vernon hospital, where he was pronounced dead.

While the shock of the event rippled throughout the campus, the body of the ill-fated student was transported to his hometown for burial. This might well have concluded the dreadful incident, except for a series of events that are rumored to have occurred in the months and years following. It is said that after the death of her boyfriend, the young woman with whom he had spent his final moments suffered from a series of horrible nightmares. In each, her deceased boyfriend visited her in her room. While such nightmares might be expected by one so close to a tragic event, so strong were these dreams that she eventually decided to move out of her room and into a new setting.

On the appointed day, she and a friend carefully moved all of her belongings out of her room and down the hall to the elevator that had played the key role in the tragedy. At the elevator the young woman realized she had inadvertently left one box in her room and asked her friend to retrieve her belongings. Accordingly, the girl's friend went back to the room and unlocked the door but found it would not budge, as though the entrance were somehow blocked by an obstruction.

Applying her full strength to the door, she felt something give way on the other side and was able to open it far enough to stick her head in the room. Much to her shock, she found that in the few moments of their absence, a heavy chest of drawers had been transported across the room and lodged directly behind the door. What made this even more chilling was the fact that no one was present inside the eighth floor room, with no window present for egress.

Since that day, residents of that room have experienced a series of unsettling occurrences. According to Chris Woodyard, in her book *Haunted Ohio,* students in the room have been awakened by the feel of icy hands caressing their faces. Others have reported glimpsing the transparent form of young man leaning prosaically against a bookcase in one corner of the room. One student, Woodyard relates, even reported that the ghost tried to smother her with her own pillow.

English Professor Tim Shutt, who is considered an authority on the ghosts of Kenyon, has been quoted as saying he has heard of the Caples ghost from several students over the years. In 1993, Shutt told the *Kenyon Collegian,* "In the past three years six students, all known to me personally, have told me tales of Caples, in which the student feels someone sit at the bedside, or someone lie on top of them, immobilizing the student." Shutt goes on to note that one striking aspect of these reports is that at least two of the students were unaware of the ghostly reputation of the building at the time of their reports.

An article in the *Kenyon Collegian* from 1988 relates that, in one week a number of years ago, several witnesses reported seeing the semitransparent form of a young man wandering the eighth floor of Caples. One girl, asleep in her room, awoke feeling a chill on her legs, as though the covers had been lifted from her. As she groggily glanced down, she was shocked into full consciousness by the sight of her blankets levitating several inches above her bed.

Another sad spirit is said to inhabit the fourth floor of Old Kenyon Hall, home to the Delta Kappa Epsilon fraternity. His story briefly took on national importance and then doomed him forever to the misty domain of college ghostlore. On October 28, 1905, at approximately 9:00 P.M., several fraternity brothers took Stuart Pierson, a pledge in the organization, from his room at Old Kenyon to take part in a part of his initiation ceremony.

While the exact intentions of the ritual are sketchy at best, is it said that Pierson was given a basket containing a mask, a length of rope and a candle and taken to the Cleveland, Akron and Columbus railroad bridge over the Kokosing River. While some variants of the legend would later state that the youth was tied to the tracks there, most accounts of the day say that he was simply told to "wait on the bridge" until summoned.

Undoubtedly, the fraternity members performing this strange ceremony felt safe in leaving the young man waiting on the tracks. Ample room on each side of the tracks would allow the young man to escape in case of the approach of a train and more to the point, no train was scheduled to cross the tracks till morning. However, events were to take a terrible turn that night, twisting what might have amounted to an episode of fraternity hazing into outright manslaughter.

The most popular theory goes that as Pierson waited on the tracks that dark evening, long hours of study and fraternity pledging took their toll. Time passed and as the obedient pledge waited, he began to succumb to a drowsy sleep.

Little did he know that at that moment, miles away, his fate was being sealed by a locomotive of the C.A.&C. railroad, which was dispatched to take a damaged freight car to Mt. Vernon for repairs. As the locomotive plunged through the darkness that night, no one on board had any idea that the sleeping form of a college freshman lay in its path. It is thought that Pierson was killed instantly when struck

Caples Hall at Kenyon College is said to house the ghost of a young man who fell eight floors to his death in an elevator shaft.

Photo: Kenyon College

that night. So quick was the event that the locomotive engineer had no idea that he had struck someone until his engine stopped in Mt. Vernon.

Meanwhile, shortly after 10 P.M., fraternity members in charge of Pierson's initiation returned to collect their ward, but found only the basket they had given him lying undisturbed next to the tracks. After a brief search, the mangled body of Pierson was found some sixty feet down the tracks from the place he had been struck.

When found, his body carried on it an ominous message. A sign, pinned to the front of his shirt by the fraternity members who had left him on the bridge read, "This will do for this time, but if we come again it will be worse." A cryptic message at best, made even more macabre by the tragedy of that night.

Ironically, Pierson's father had traveled from Cincinnati that night to be a part of his son's formal initiation the next evening. As an alumnus of both Kenyon College and Delta Kappa Epsilon, he was looking forward to watching as his son followed in his footsteps attaining membership in the fraternity. Instead, early the next morning he was awakened by the horrendous news of his son's demise. After viewing the battered remains of his son's body, the elder Mr. Pierson had it loaded on a freight car and transported back to Cincinnati for burial.

Almost immediately after word of the death leaked out, it created a national furor. Since the existence of Greek organizations was still held suspect by the public at the time, Pierson's death caused much debate across the country regarding the value of fraternities and sororities on campus. In particular, as the first hazing related death in America, the dangers of initiation practices and hazing were brought to national attention for the first time.

Meanwhile, life slowly reverted to normal at the Kenyon College. Strict new guidelines were instituted for fraternities and sororities. and the gruesome death of Stuart Pierson became just another footnote in the annals of campus history, overlooked and forgotten.

Forgotten, perhaps, except for the strange and foreboding events that are said to occur on the fourth floor of Old Kenyon Hall. For many years, it has been said that on October 28, the anniversary of the mishap, the face of a young man has been glimpsed gazing out at the campus from the round "bullseye" window of the building. Behind that window, some suggest, is the very room from which Stuart Pierson was taken to meet his dreadful fate. One story told for years at Kenyon states that as the face appears at the window, the sound of a phantom locomotive can heard thundering across the now infamous railroad trestle in the distance.

Inside the fourth floor, the residence of the Delta Kappa Epsilon fraternity is also said to be the site of strange occurrences. Doors open and shut of their own accord and lights flicker for no apparent reason. Windows have been seen to open despite the fact that no human agency was responsible for the movement. Perhaps most interestingly, fraternity members have routinely reported the sound of footsteps moving up and down on the floor above them. In fact, the building only has four floors, and the walkway above the fourth floor is an attic, where the entrance been boarded over for many years.

Like many of the spirits at Kenyon, the shade of Stuart Pierson has gone on to become a part of the cherished lore at the campus. His life and death have become as much a part of the fabric of tradition at Kenyon College as midterm examinations and homecoming dances. As student Bertram Tunnell notes in an article concerning Pierson's death in the *Kenyon Collegian,* "Stuart Pierson is a grim reminder of our own mortality in the little crystal bubble that is Kenyon College."

While the tragic events that gave birth to the ghost stories concerning the Delta Kappa Epsilon fraternity and Caples Hall have cast their dark shadow across the college, they pale in comparison with the traumatic events of February 27, 1949. It was in the early morning hours of that terrible day that nine young men lost their lives in a fire at Old Kenyon dormitory.

That Saturday night began peacefully for the residents of the hall. The second semester was well under way, and the residents of Old Kenyon were enjoying a small fire in the fireplace located in the parlor on the first floor. The evening had seen the annual sophomore dance at the Rosse Hall Annex, and some of the residents of Old Kenyon had brought their dates back to the dormitory for refreshments. By 2:30 A.M., the fire in the grate had burned to embers, the last of the dates had departed, and most of the men had gone to bed for the night.

At 3:35 that morning, watchman Emerson Billman entered the building to make sure all was well. He would later recalled seeing only a few men sitting in the parlor before the ashes of their fire, but nothing else of note. Touring the rest of the building, Billman left the building at about 4:00 A.M. to continue his rounds.

Just ten minutes later, after leaving Mather Hall, the watchman walked back through campus past Old Kenyon. As he came within sight of the dormitory, a horrifying sight confronted him. Flames had erupted in Old Kenyon, already engulfing the second, third and fourth floors.

Later investigation conjectured that sparks from the fire in the parlor fireplace had gone up the chimney and then settled back into an old flue, lodging in an opening between floors. After smoldering for some hours, the sparks erupted into flame and the entire building quickly became an inferno. Although most of the students were able to escape from the main entrance of the building or jumped to safety from windows, some caught in the upper floors of the building had no chance of survival.

Indeed, poignant stories from the time relate that as the flames reached their height, singing was heard from within the inferno, as students caught in the flames and smoke, realizing the impossibility of escape, chose to exit this life in song.

All through the night, fire fighters from Gambier and surrounding comminutes fought the blaze in vain. By dawn the next day, the building was reduced to smoking ruin. All told, nine students lost their lives in the fire. Six of the young men had been trapped in their fourth floor rooms and perished there. Two young men died while attempting to jump to safety from upper story windows, and one young man died the next day at a Mt. Vernon hospital of extensive burns and smoke inhalation.

The trauma of the Old Kenyon fire shook the college to its very foundations. Classes were suspended for a week as the campus struggled to deal with the death of nine of its members, and students went into open mourning.

In the wake of the devastation, it was announced that Old Kenyon would be rebuilt "stone by stone and piece by piece" as a nearly exact replica of the dormitory that had been destroyed. Photos of the dormitory were collected to serve as a model for the new building, and stones from the original construction were painstakingly salvaged from the ruin and numbered for use in the new structure.

Significantly, however, the one change that was made to the new building was the decision to raise the foundation level some ten inches from the original. This seemingly minor detail would later play a role in the strange tales that would come to center around the new building. For, as the years have passed, it has become commonly accepted on the campus that the spirits of the nine young men who lost their lives in the fire haunt the "new" Old Kenyon Hall.

One student who lived for a year in a room that corresponded to that of a young man who had died in the fire, reported waking up one night to hear his closet door shaking, as though someone inside were struggling to escape. At that moment, according to the story, a hollow voice from inside the closet was heard to gasp, "Get me out!" Of course, an inspection of the closet proved it empty. This story is embellished with the rumor that one of the young men who had died in the fire was found afterward in his closet, where he had retreated from the smoke and flames.

Another student, studying in his room late one night, was shocked when he felt someone touch his shoulder and a voice in his ear demanded, "What are you doing in my room?" Turning quickly in the direction of the voice, the young man found that he was alone.

Still another student who lived on the fourth floor of Kenyon related the experience of being shaken awake late one night and a voice calling out, "Ed, wake up... FIRE!" This experience is chilling because, while the young man in question was not named Ed, it is true that one of the students who died in the fire was named Edward Brout.

Other students have reported the shock of being awakened at night by being violently shaken and at least one is said to have been roused from sleep by the feeling of a hand sliding along his pillow. It is also told that a security guard, checking on Old Kenyon one summer when the dormitory was supposed to be vacant, was surprised to hear the door to an empty room open and close again immediately after his departure. The same security guard later reported in an interview with student Heather Frost that while visiting one floor of Old Kenyon, he distinctly heard the sound of a shower running in one of the floor bathrooms. Since there was supposed to be no one in the dormitory, he went to the bathroom, only to find it empty except for water splashed on the floor.

An even more bizarre event occurred on February 28, 1979, the thirtieth anniversary of the catastrophe. According to several reports, on that night a student in Old Kenyon entered his room to find a single candle burning before a copy of the 1949 college yearbook. Even stranger than the fact that door had been locked prior to his entering was the fact that the neither the candle nor the yearbook belonged to the person who was staying in the room. Moreover, the yearbook was turned to a "In Memoriam" page dedicated to those who died in the fire at Old Kenyon.

One of the more intriguing tales told of Old Kenyon has been the sighting of what have been called "legless apparitions." It is said that on more than a few occasions over the years, students have reported seeing strange figures of men in floating through the hallways of the dormitory late at night. Of course, the sighting of strange young men in the dress of several decades ago prowling through the hallways of a modern dormitory at night is enough to raise some question. However, in this case there are two intriguing aspects to these sightings.

First, the young men in question were semi-transparent. Universally, students observing the visits of these figures stated that they could see through them and into the hallway beyond. Even more extraordinary, however, is the fact that these figures were partially legless. Their form, according to reports, began slightly below their knees, which were at the level of the floor. This was the view from above. According to Professor Timothy Shutt, who heard the story from students when he first came to the college some years ago, those viewing the spirits from the floor below were treated to an even more bizarre sight. Writing in the *Kenyon Collegian*, Shutt related that students unfortunate enough to be positioned beneath such a specter were treated to the sight of disembodied calves and feet "hanging like stalagmites" from their ceilings.

These observations caused much wonder and speculation on campus, until records of the reconstruction of Old Kenyon were examined, and it was recalled that when the dormitory was rebuilt after the calamitous fire, its level was raised about ten inches. Thus, it is said that whatever shades were walking the halls of Old Kenyon were doing so on the original floor level, as though walking on floorboards that had long ago been destroyed.

And so it seems to go at Kenyon College. From one end of this seemingly serene campus to the other, stories of spooks and specters are in plentiful supply. So abundant are the supernatural tales at this campus that the college archives has developed an actual "ghost file" of nearly a hundred pages. Every year the campus newspaper retells the stories, so that new and old and freshmen entering the college are soon indoctrinated with the tales of its resident apparitions.

Speaking with college historians, faculty and students, it is easy to sense the sense of pride that Kenyon College maintains in its resident ghostlore. The legends and perhaps even the ghosts themselves are a valued and cherished part of the character of this extraordinary college.

While it must be noted that a tour of campus does not feature the gates to hell itself and there is little here to substantiate the label of "the most evil place on earth," still the aura of the old tales surrounding the college are a tangible part of the fabric of life there. While other colleges and universities might also wish to lay claim to the title of "the most haunted university in the U.S.," none seems to take as much real pride in its spectral residents than does Kenyon College.

12

When Hell Came to Pennsylvania
Gettysburg College
Gettysburg, Pennsylvania

The regiments passing to the front marched not between festoons of the ladies' smiles and waving handkerchiefs, thrown kisses and banner presentations. They were looked upon sadly and in a certain awe, as those who had taken on themselves a doom. The muster rolls on which the name and oath were written were pledges of honor, redeemable at the gates of death.

Major General Joshua L. Chamberlain

The battle of Gettysburg marked the terrible climax to the most bloody war in America's history. Perhaps no other moment before or since has so captured the pathos and tragedy of war. In three days of unimaginable bloodshed and carnage, over seven thousand young men lost their lives, their bodies strewn across the pastoral Pennsylvania landscape. Another forty-four thousand would be wounded, captured or listed as missing in action. Whole divisions were mowed down by artillery barrage and musket fire. As one survivor later recalled, "The battlefield looked like hell had come to earth."

The battle of Gettysburg is generally regarded by historians to be the turning point of the Civil War. While some point out that Gettysburg was but one of several key battles that sealed the fate of the Southern cause, still the horrendous impact of these three days of battle cannot be underestimated.

In the ensuing years, the Civil War, and particularly the battle of Gettysburg, has caught the imagination of America. Names such as "The Wheatfield," "Little Roundtop," and the infamous "Pickett's Charge" have become indelibly etched into our national consciousness.

Ironically, the battle itself was never meant to happen. The first years of the Civil War went disastrously for the Union forces. Although possessing a larger and better-equipped army, the Union suffered from inadequate leadership, resulting in bloody defeats at Manassas, Fredericksberg, and Chancellorsville.

In early 1863, emboldened by his initial successes and the possibility of England recognizing the Confederacy as a independent nation, General Robert E. Lee decided to take the battle to the Union on its own territory. Lee headed north with the largest Confederate army ever assembled—some seventy-three thousand men. His initial objective was Harrisburg, Pennsylvania, where he planned to cut the single railroad link to the Midwest, thus severing the flow of Union reinforcements from that direction. It is thought that it was Lee's plan to then capture Philadelphia. Perhaps he hoped that the capture of a major northern city would entice Great Britain to intervene and negotiate a peace.

In early June the Southern army moved north from southern Virginia through the Shenandoah Valley and into western Maryland. Lee then turned his army west into Pennsylvania. Sending his vaunted Confederate cavalry forward, led by commander Jeb Stuart, to insulate his army from the northern forces, Lee moved through Pennsylvania toward his goal of Harrisburg. It was his wish to avoid any major engagements prior to reaching Harrisburg, fearing that any battle might slow or even stop his progress.

However, on July 1, his fears were realized. On that day the vanguard of Lee's army reached the sleepy town of Gettysburg, where six strategic roads intersected. At dawn a Union cavalry patrol under the command of General John Buford encountered the leading elements of the Confederate army just west of the town. After a brief skirmish, both sides retreated and called for reinforcements.

The first day's battle was judged a success for the Confederacy. Attempting to force a quick retreat by the Union, General Harry Heth sent wave after wave of his infantry against a Union force outnumbered roughly four to one.

Armed with Spencer repeating rifles, which shot up to six times faster than the muskets carried by the Confederates, the Union forces exacted a heavy toll of casualties from the Confederates. However, at the end of the day, Union troops were forced to retreat through the town to take up a defensive position on the high ground just south of Gettysburg.

During the night, large numbers of reinforcements arrived from both sides, and by the next morning it was obvious that a major battle was imminent. All that day the Union army, still outnumbered, managed to hold its position on a ridge of high ground running from Culp's Hill, just south and east of town, south to a hill known as Little Round Top. Both forces brought forward the full brunt of their artillery, and throughout the day the armies exchanged cannon barrages punctuated by infantry charges.

By that night, the countryside was littered with the dead and dying, yet the Union forces retained their positions south of Gettysburg. At this point, the battle had been fought to a near-draw. It might have remained so, with no clear victor, had not General Lee made an uncharacteristic and ultimately disastrous decision.

Erroneously believing that the Union had reinforced its left and right flanks at the expense of the middle of its line, Lee ordered an attack directly up the middle of the Union line, to be preceded by an artillery barrage of several hours. He hoped to shatter the center of the Union defenses and send the federal army into full retreat. It was a bold and even desperate move, on which the hopes of the battle and perhaps even the war were pinned. For this fated attack, Lee chose three of his most trusted commanders—General William Pender, General James Pettigrew, and General George Pickett, whose name would be forever linked to the calamity of the next day.

What followed was unimaginable carnage. In the midafternoon, over fifteen thousand men wearing the gray of the Confederacy stepped out from their positions and began a charge uphill toward the Union lines. Against them were six thousand veteran Union soldiers, led by a man who has been called one of the greatest commanders of the war, General John Gibbon.

Despite what later dramatic histories may have portrayed, in truth the attack never stood a chance. Of the fifteen thousand Confederate troops who charged toward the middle of the Union line that day, only about two hundred reached the copse of trees that was to serve as the axis of attack. Of those who did make it, few ever lived to retreat back to their own lines.

When the charge was over, roughly two-thirds of the attacking Confederates were dead, wounded or captured. In places the dead lay in piles four deep. The blood of both attackers and defenders flowed like grisly rivers, dampening the ground like unholy dew.

Pickett's Charge, and indeed the entire battle, ended as a disastrous defeat for the Confederacy. On July 4, as America recognized the eighty-seventh anniversary of its birth, the Confederate army retreated south toward the Potomac River, leaving the remains of thousands of its young men behind. With those young men, General Lee was also leaving behind his best hope for Southern independence.

All told, Lee had lost twenty thousand men, more than a third of his army. While the Union would claim Gettysburg as a major victory, the federal army would count twenty-three thousand of its men dead and wounded. For both armies, and for the entire nation as well, the battle was a wrenching, catastrophic event.

In the aftermath of the battle, the townspeople of Gettysburg were forced to view a surreal landscape. Bodies and dismembered limbs littered the battlefield and town. Many of the buildings in the town not damaged by the fighting were immediately pressed into use as impromptu morgues. So numerous were the casualties that at first farmers simply buried the dead in large unmarked graves in farm fields. The mounds marking the soldiers' eternal rest gradually meshed with the surrounding earth.

While there remained nearly two years of war yet to be fought, the battle of Gettysburg would ultimately toll the death knell of the Confederacy. Lee would never again be able to turn his armies north and, instead, was occupied for the rest of the war with defending his Southern homeland from encroaching northern armies.

The battle of Gettysburg marked a seminal point in the Civil War in more ways than one. As historian J. P. Wilkins noted,

> The battle of Gettysburg is the single episode which stole the Victorian adventure and glamour from the war for both sides. No more fighting was done that year . . . The next battles [i.e., Grant and Lee in the Wilderness in May 1864] saw experienced troops on both sides refusing to attack, or retreating with only the slightest show of resistance. Except for the Wilderness, the rebel forces in the east would never again attack in force. Gettysburg indelibly taught both sides the true horrors of war.

If ever there was an event in American history that created the kind of spiritual trauma said to produce ghostly phenomena, then the battle of Gettysburg is surely that event. Long after the last of the combatants withdrew from the bloodied battlefield, the events that occurred there continued to have historical and national repercussions. However, in the once-sleepy little town of Gettysburg, it is said that the battle has had other consequences as well—strange echoes of a time when the nation's turmoil boiled and raged, and for a short while, hell came to Pennsylvania.

Over the years a legion of ghost stories has become associated with the Gettysburg battleground—extraordinary tales that encompass much of the battlefield and also the town itself. Many of these tales have been carefully collected and retold by Mark Nesbitt, a local author, historian and former National Park Service employee. In three fascinating books on the ghosts of Gettysburg, Nesbitt tells of the spectral inhabitants of the area. In these three volumes most of the ghostly tales are compiled, and from these books are drawn the stories told here.

Gettysburg College stands sedate and tranquil amid the rolling plains of central Pennsylvania. Viewing the college today, it is hard to imagine that the school itself was once embroiled in the life and death struggle that has forever marked the ground of Gettysburg as hallowed. Gettysburg College, once known as Pennsylvania College, was chartered in 1832, before the area became enmeshed in the strife between the north and south. Though the campus has grown enormously in recent years, at the time of the battle of Gettysburg the college consisted of three brick buildings, providing lodging and educational facilities for little more than a hundred students.

When the War Between the States erupted so violently around this once-serene institution, the area around the college, like much of the town, was the scene of violent battle. During and after the conflict, the college buildings were compelled into use as a a refuge for the wounded and dying. While some of these building have since been torn down and replaced, still the college itself is said to bear the spiritual marks of their presence and of the violent events that embroiled them. Not one but several building on campus are said to be haunted by remnants of the past at Gettysburg College. As one might guess, many of these have their origins in the events of July, 1863.

One of the most enduring legends handed down through the generations at Gettysburg College is that of Pennsylvania Hall, a stately white-columned structure which once served as a student dormitory and now houses the administrative offices for the college. Erected in 1837, Pennsylvania Hall, or Old Dorm as it is known, was one of the first buildings constructed on campus. Large and expansive for its time, the building served as living quarters for university students for many years before the onset of the Civil War. Actually, during the battle itself, it was the very size of the building which attracted the attention of the Confederate army, which immediately occupied it for use as a makeshift hospital .

Even today, the horror of battlefield conflict can reduce medical care to its lowest possible denominator, but hospital conditions at that time made caring for the wounded an even more grisly and often futile task. As Nesbitt describes the scene in his book, *Ghosts of Gettysburg:*

Photo: Troy Taylor

Old Dorm at Gettysburg College is rumored to house the ghosts of Civil War soldiers.

> Nearly every wound to extremity resulted in an amputation. With hundreds of torn bodies pouring into the facility every hour, careful setting of the bone was impossible. An amputation could be performed in just a few minutes. The limb…was tossed ignominiously out the nearest window, to tangle sickeningly with the hideous pyramid of arms, legs, feet and hands growing below the sill.

As wrenching as such a description might seem, it does not begin to explain the full horror of the scene that surrounded Pennsylvania Hall during the battle. According to descriptions at the time, blood splattered the walls and floor of the operating room and the air was filled with the screams of human agony as surgeons operated without benefit of anesthesia.

Outside the hall, a roped-off area was reserved for those who, chiefly due to head or abdominal injury, were too far gone for medical treatment. Here these hapless souls lay exposed to the elements, their mangled bodies twitching and tortured eyes pleading simply for death.

In this grimmest of settings, doctors and surgeons worked for three days, most often in vain, to save the lives of those that war had horribly mutilated. Meanwhile, above the suffering and pain, but by no means immune to it, Confederate General Robert E. Lee stood in the cupola of Old Dorm, watching the progress of the battle going on around him. Perhaps, as some might suggest, he watches still.

It is said that on certain nights, members of the campus community have reported seeing the figures of men anxiously pacing back and forth in the tower of Pennsylvania Hall. While the descriptions vary, most often they are described as resembling the sentries that were stationed with Lee to guard his safety and deliver messages to the battlefront. Occasionally it is said that General Lee himself is seen at the height of the tower, looking down at the now-quiet countryside just as he did during the battle.

One student reported in a paper submitted to Professor Charles Emmons that he had seen this apparition not once but several times. The student, writing for a sociology project, reported that while living in a dormitory room just fifty yards from Pennsylvania Hall, he and a roommate had seen a figure in the tower of the hall several nights in a row. Further, he added, at the time of the sighting, the figure was gesturing wildly. Thinking at first that someone might have inadvertently been trapped in the tower, both young men ran to the steps of the building and shouted to the figure, only to have him disappear suddenly. Subsequent investigation by campus security proved the building empty.

Other reports indicate the sighting of not one but several figures standing in the small chamber atop the tower. One student even claimed that two of the figures carried Civil War vintage muskets on their shoulders: old sentries, perhaps, keeping their eternal vigil.

Over the years, a great many students have reported seeing the spectral figure or figures in the cupola of Pennsylvania Hall. However, theirs is by no means the only ghostly presence to reside unquietly within those hallowed walls. Indeed, if the story told of an experience shared by two college administrators not long ago is true, then something even more dark and dreadful might still lurk within the dark recesses of the building.

According to Nesbitt, the story is told that one night two college administrators who had been working late on the fourth floor entered the elevator. However, instead of going to the first floor as they intended, the pair was surprised when the elevator descended past the first floor and on down to the basement level. Thinking they had inadvertently pushed the wrong button, one of the men was reaching to push the button for the first floor when the elevator doors opened to a horrifying scene.

Gone was the basement floor as they knew it, filled with storage boxes and crates. Instead, before them they saw a blood-spattered operating room from a century before. Casualties wearing the gray of the Confederacy littered the floor, while amongst them a ghostly contingent of medical personnel moved silently. As Nesbitt relates the story:

> . . . the blood-stained doctors and orderlies . . . again were performing their abhorrent and hideous tasks of slicing sinew and sawing bone . . . suturing arteries and tying ligaments. Armloads of severed limbs [were being carried] to grisly, blood-dampened corners and unceremoniously dumped.

Frantically, one of the administrators punched the elevator's buttons, trying to end the captivation of the awful scene before them. In a moment, the elevator doors did indeed begin to close, but not before one of the incorporeal orderlies turned and looked at them imploringly, as though asking for their help to escape his endless gruesome work.

To their credit, both administrators are said to have continued to work in Pennsylvania Hall even after their traumatic experience. However, when staying late into the evening, both chose the stairs as their means of departure—best, perhaps, to avoid even the possibility of contact with the awful secrets of Old Dorm.

There is yet another brief, unsettling footnote told regarding the valiant doctors of Pennsylvania Hall. After their terrible work was done, reports indicate that bodies and parts of bodies lay strewn both inside and outside the building like ghastly debris. Following the battle, bodies and limbs were gathered for disposal and, since no local cemetery was large enough to accommodate the enormous influx of the dead, many of the human remains were taken to a nearby area known as Stein Lake.

In fact, this name was somewhat misleading, since the area was not a lake, but simply a low-lying area adjacent to campus that frequently flooded after a hard rain. Since the earth there was soft and moist, making for easy digging, a huge pit was dug there. Bodies, whole and in parts, were simply thrown in and the hollow covered over. Some years later, when the national cemetery was consecrated in the battlefield area, Stein Lake was excavated and at least some of the bodies were exhumed for reburial. Even at the time, however, it was said that to remove all the bodies was impossible. Specifically, while the removal of many bodies from Stein Lake was well documented, no record exists of the removal of the thousands of severed human limbs that had been placed there.

After the last of the recovered bodies had been reburied, Stein Lake reverted to its natural state of quiet solitude until the 1970s, when it was announced that Gettysburg College would excavate the area and build a new library. Students would soon study in quiet above the soil where the quiet dead had once laid in repose.

Bulldozers and excavating machinery rumbled in, and the land was disturbed as tons of new earth were added to raise the level of the land for the library foundation. At this point, some say, the quiet dead became not so quiet. Almost from the first, stories suggest that the construction project seemed jinxed. Machinery broke down constantly and tools were said to disappear from plain view. More startling still were the sounds of human groaning and anguish which seemed to issue from the very ground upon which the workmen toiled.

Finally, as legend has it, the workmen went to the supervisor and asked that a minister be brought to the site for a special blessing before they could continue their work. While it is not known if the request was granted, eventually the work did continue and today, Musselman Library stands proudly and placidly on the land once occupied by Stein Lake.

However, even to this day, rumors persist that library staff working late at night will hear sighs and even low moans echoing through the dark corridors. While some might pass off these errant sounds as the customary noises associated with water pipes and heating vents, still some wonder if, deep below the foundation of Musselman Library, dark graves of the forgotten men who gave their lives in battle might be troubled, as spirits cry out for the recognition denied them.

Meanwhile all across campus, other spirits of the unquiet dead are said to walk. The fact that Gettysburg College and many of its facilities were used as impromptu medical facilities by both sides during and after the battle has given rise to another legend associated with the College Health Service building

While the building itself is of fairly recent vintage, the land on which it resides once witnessed the carnage associated with the battle. Here the Union Army retreated in disarray during the initial stages of the conflict. Young men from Maine, Pennsylvania and Massachusetts, many stained with the blood of battle, limped back from the atrocity of war toward the Mummasburg Road. Many did not make it and fell from their wounds in the vicinity where now stands a facility dedicated to the health and welfare of young people.

Perhaps this is why, as Mr. Nesbitt relates, there are recurrent rumors of a "presence" in the Health Service building. Odd noises are often heard in the middle of the night and phantom footsteps are noticed padding the halls when no one is in the facility.

One nurse who worked nights in the center in the mid 1980s told Nesbitt of a great many experiences with the phantom presence of the Health Center. As Nesbitt describes it, the woman recalled:

> Alone in the semi-darkened Health Center at night, she would often hear footfalls coming down the hall toward the nurse's office. She would leave her desk and try and help whatever student had gotten up to wander the halls, but no invariably one was there. The only times that the sounds of the footsteps were frightening were when she knew that no one was checked into the center that night. Those times she called College Security, who came promptly but found no one to arrest.

The nurse in question also told Nesbitt that other odd occurrences were common as well. Frequently, photos were known to fall off the walls of vacant rooms. These would be carefully replaced, only to fall off again an hour or so later. Inspection of the wall and nail behind the picture offered no explanation for the events.

Covers were frequently flung from radiators when no living person was in the vicinity. What made these phenomena even more odd was the fact that they would sometimes occur eight or ten times during the course of a night. So commonplace did these strange occurrences become that the nurse said she eventually learned to simply turn up the volume of the television at her desk and ignore them while doing paperwork.

Like others who have worked in the Health Center, the nurse reported that her time there was constantly filled with the feeling that "someone else was around"—an unseen resident, neither malevolent nor evil but simply an ever present part of the atmosphere in the building. Somewhat prosaically, she speculated to the author that it might be the spirit of one of the casualties of the battle coming back to check on the welfare of other young people, perhaps wishing to convey some manner of comfort denied him in his moment of death.

Other spirits associated with the university, however, do not seem so benevolent. Glatfelter Hall, an imposing brick building with a looming bell tower that seems to brood over the campus, is said to be inhabited by a female apparition. According to Mark Nesbitt in his *Ghosts of Gettysburg,* legend suggests that on numerous occasions the figure, dressed in Victorian garb, has been seen in the upper area of the bell tower beckoning to young men passing by below.

Nesbitt relates that this figure is said to be that of a local young woman who lost her lover in the battle. According to the tale, the young woman was brokenhearted by his death. The ill fated girl is said to have mourned for many years until, driven to distraction by her grief, she climbed to the bell tower of Glatfelter Hall and ended her life in violent free fall.

Today, tradition suggests that male students passing by the Glatfelter hall on moonlit evenings have seen the eerie form of the woman looking down at them from the recesses of the bell tower, beckoning to them in a pleading and almost pathetic way. While there is no record of a student complying with her unspoken request, still the story suggests that she is attempting to lure them to share in her unhappy fate. Like the sirens of old, perhaps she is trying to lure them to their doom, enticing them to join her in death and share in her unhappy fate.

. No self-respecting college theater is complete without a resident ghost story, and Gettysburg College is no exception. Brua Hall, which houses both the central theater for the campus and a smaller auditorium known at Stevens Theater, is said to be haunted by a specter known as "the General."

Brua Hall was constructed in 1889, fully twenty-six years after the battle of Gettysburg. However, at least one professor has posited the belief that the structure was built over the site of a temporary Civil War burial ground. Such a supposition might well be accurate, since a great many fields surrounding the campus and town were used for this purpose immediately after the battle. Several years later, when more formal and suitable cemeteries were established to memorialize the dead, bodies were disinterred from their temporary resting places. However, it is widely believed that in the process many bodies were left behind, since decomposition and poor record keeping at the time of burial kept workers from knowing how many bodies had been interred at a given location. Perhaps, if this theory is true, it might well explain the phantom presence which has for years made itself known in the precincts of Brua Hall.

Brua Hall is a striking structure both in history and architecture. Built as the chapel for the campus, the exterior features a tall bell tower and twin bronze turrets, giving the structure a medieval look. Inside, a high gabled ceiling overlooks stone walls and ornate wooden latticework. Due to its renovation from chapel to theater complex, the building's interior is catacombed with false entrances, trap doors and labyrinthine passageways. From the height of the metal grid system over the stage down to the dark "catacombs" of the basement, the building is filled with an eerie murkiness and strange shadows that seem to float down empty passageways.

In such a setting, it would be a disappointment if this this foreboding edifice did not have at least one ghost story of which to boast. In the case of Brua Hall, there is no such disappointment, since its ghosts are a well established legend on campus.

"The General," as he is popularly called, has been an accepted feature in the theater for a number of years. Through the passing generations of students, tales of him have been handed down, perhaps embellished and magnified with each telling.

Beneath the veneer of legend and fable, however, lies a core of truly inexplicable experiences frequently reported at Brua Hall. One of the places in which students have reported encountering this unseen presence is in an angled passageway that leads between the dressing rooms and stage left in Kline Theater. Always kept dark during performances, it is through this passageway that student actors must pass in order to arrive at their prescribed locations on stage in time for their cues. However, over the years, more than a few students have reported bumping into someone in the narrow twisting passage. Though unseen in the dark, the figure seems solid enough, until further investigation reveals the corridor empty.

The General does not limit his activities to this particular walkway, however. According to Mark Nesbitt, the ghostly phantom has been seen and felt throughout the building. One of the first encounters with the shade occurred some years ago and resulted in his name. According to campus legend, several students were working late one night on the stage, which was partially set up for an upcoming production. A single chair sat at the center of the stage, while the two students labored at hanging props from the metal grid system overhead. In order to accomplish this task, one student stood atop a tall ladder near the front of the stage, while his coworker traipsed back and forth from the backstage area, handing up the props to be hung.

After one trip from backstage, the student reached up to hand a prop to his coworker on the ladder, only to see him staring down at the stage below, a look of glazed terror on his face. As the student at the lower end of the ladder turned toward the direction of his friend's gaze, he was shocked to see the figure of a elderly gentleman, dressed in the uniform of a Union officer, nonchalantly reclining on the one seat on stage. According to the story recounted by Nesbitt, the two students looked at each other in dumb disbelief for a moment and when they looked back at the stage, it was empty.

If this was the first sighting of the spirit of Brua Hall, it would by no means be the last. Since then, it is said that passersby late at night have seen the face of a man peering down at them from the high arched windows on the east side of the building. What makes such an appearance especially noteworthy is the fact that those windows have been covered over from the inside for many years.

It is also said that the General has shown a propensity for certain young female performers. More than one actress, during a performance, is said to have been forced to struggle to stay in character when, looking into the house seats, she observed the figure of a gentleman in Civil War garb seated in the auditorium. According to the tales, he is seen enjoying the performance amid an audience that seems oblivious to his presence.

Nesbitt also reports that the sound of phantom footsteps crossing the stage is so common that students accustomed to working in the area accept them as simply part of the scenery. For some reason, the steps are generally heard climbing the steps to the stage right area. As one theater major has said, "It is kind of an initiation—the first time you hear the steps and see that no one is there, it is disconcerting, but then you realize that the General has accepted you being there. It is sort of like you belong after that."

One student who reported an experience with the ghost of the General was Carole Herman, a theater and philosophy major who reported to Nesbitt that she had caught a glimpse of the General one winter night while working in the theater. As she was setting up props for an upcoming production, she noticed a movement behind the glass windows of the lighting booth at the back of the theater.

Although the room was darkened, she could clearly see a figure moving back and forth in the room, despite the fact that Carole had not heard the door to the booth open, and the only other occupant of the theater was a student working backstage. After a few moments the form seemed to disappear from view, despite the fact that no one had left the room through the one door leading to it.

In fact, working in the theater over a number of years, Carole Herman seems to have developed a certain feeling toward whatever inhabits the old building. She is quoted as having said that she has felt not one, but two spirits in the stage area, one male and one female. Though their presence might be subtle, "You can tell when they are here and when they're not," she told Nesbitt.

Carole Herman's report of seeing "something" in the lighting booth is not the only such sighting. Frequently, students have reported strange flickering lights and shapes in the booth, sometimes called the control room. Interestingly, these sightings are often accompanied by lights that seem to dim, flash, and even turn themselves on of their own volition. When these odd phenomena occur, students are inclined to simply shrug off the incidents as "the General at work."

The peculiar goings on at Brua do not limit themselves to Kline Theater. Other strange occurrences have been reported in Stevens Theater, a small auditorium just behind Kline. According to legend, a student was once relegated to the job of moving chairs from Stevens Theater to Kline to provide extra seating for a play to begin the next night. After making what she thought was her last trip between the two theaters, the student realized that one chair had been left behind in Stevens. Somewhat reluctantly, the student returned. As she bent to pick up the chair in the empty theater, a cold, clear voice rang out through the dark air: "Oh, I *thought* you were supposed to pick up that chair."

Unnerved, the girl called out, demanding to know who was there, but only silence reigned in the dark theater. Now, more curious than afraid, she searched the small theater, but found all the doors locked and the stage and seating area devoid of human habitation.

It is also in Stevens that the ghost has shown a preoccupation with rearranging props. On more than one occasion, props left overnight have been found rearranged or moved during the night, despite the fact that the theater has been empty in the interim. On at least on occasion, a table was set up on center stage with props adorning the paper covered surface. As is common in theater productions, each prop was carefully outlined on the table covering in magic marker to allow for easy replacement between shows.

The evening of the dress rehearsal, after the props were set and outlined, the theater was locked tightly for the night. When the stage manager reentered the next day in preparation for the performance, he saw, as he expected, that the props left on the table were in their proper positions. However, on closer inspection he noticed something bizarre. Though the props were in their proper locations on the table, the outlines on the paper covering had been shifted. It was almost, he later surmised, as though all the objects on the table had been levitated and the tablecloth shifted ninety degrees—though the auditorium had been locked and empty since the night before.

More and more stories surface regarding Brua Hall each year. Nesbitt recounts that after his visit to the theater while doing research for his *Ghosts of Gettysburg,* a student called to report that ever since the author had left, a water faucet in the stage area had begun to turn itself on and off again and again.

Although some of the incidents reported seem minor in and of themselves, placed together they form the mosaic of a classically haunted theater. Some might pass off the stories as mere theater superstition, but for the students who work in and around Brua Hall, the presence of the General is an accepted part of life there.

As can be seen, most of the ghostly stories attached to Gettysburg College find their origin in the great battle that was fought there. In fact, it is understandable that such a traumatic event would give birth to a host of such tales. Interestingly, however, one of the best known and well documented ghost stories told of the school seemingly bears no connection to the battle.

The stories of Stevens Hall and the infamous "Blue Boy" who is said to inhabit the third floor there have been told for many years on campus. So well circulated are the stories that they have become part of the very fabric of the college's tradition and folklore. In truth, there is said to be not one but several ghosts inhabiting the third floor of Stevens Hall. Though differing in appearance and in the manifestations they are said to perpetrate, all apparently are the shades of young people, ranging in age from childhood to about twenty.

It is unclear how these legends of young spirits have become attached to Stevens Hall. Long-held college lore states that the third floor was once used to house orphaned and disadvantaged children, yet there is no historical record of this. However, it is known that from 1911 to 1935 the building was used as an adjunct preparatory school for the college and, as such, housed young people of high school age and below.

Perhaps it is from this period that the stories of the youthful phantoms of Stevens Hall take their root. As the Mark Nesbitt puts it:

> Wherever they come from, whether based in historical fact or not, there are persistent stories of sightings of reembodied children and young women appearing on the third floor, seeking some of the things that were denied them in life, looking, forever, for something still missing.

Indeed this seems to be the case. One of the most frequently reported sightings is that of a spectral young woman who seems to have little respect for the privacy or property of others. Her presence has been reported any number of times throughout the last decades.

According to legend, not so many years ago a female student unlocked the door to her third floor room late one night after a date. Expecting to find the room empty, as her roommate was away for the weekend, she was shocked to turn on the overhead light and see the figure of a strange young woman who looked to be about sixteen standing before a mirror in the room, apparently admiring herself. Stranger still, before the student could ask the intruder what she was doing in her room, the figure turned and fled into the closet next to the mirror.

Not sure now if she should call Campus Security or confront the prowler, the young coed slowly walked over to the closet and opened the door, but could find no evidence of the girl who had entered it just a moment before. A brief search behind the clothes and boxes revealed the wardrobe to be empty. The intruder had simply vanished.

As startling as this young student's experience may have been, her feelings of having her living space invaded pale in comparison with those of another young woman some years later. She too returned to her room on the third floor of Stevens to find a strange young woman busily pulling clothes out of a closet and holding them up to her slender frame, as though deciding which one to try on next. A cry of alarm from the room's occupant once again sent the extraordinary figure into the clothes closet where, of course, she could not be found a moment later. It seems that this strange phantom, struck by the "fashion bug," had made yet another appearance.

Over time this young female spirit has been blamed for a number of disturbances on the third floor. More than one coed has reported coming into her room to find that her clothes have been unceremoniously dumped out of her closet. One young lady, working late on a term paper, was disconcerted to hear a noise coming from the interior of her closet. Cautiously, she crept to the closet door and opened it. She saw the hangers being shaken as though someone was riffling through them. As though to complete the scene, as the girl watched in numb disbelief, one dress seemed to float off the hanger, stand sus-

Photo: Troy Taylor

A female ghost may haunt the hallways of Stevens Hall on the Gettysburg campus.

pended in thin air for a moment, and then crumple to the closet floor. Understandably, the coed ran from the room and spent the night sleeping on a friend's floor.

Other spirits have spawned legends about Stevens Hall. Another particular room on the third floor is said to be inhabited by the spirit of a young man who appears to be in his early twenties, or would be if he were counted among the living. Mark Nesbitt reports that in early 1977, a woman living in the room was alone there when something in the corner of the room caught her eye. Turning, she was startled to see the form of a young man shape itself out of the night air. Although that corner of the room was nearly dark, the student later recalled that the semitransparent figure seem to glow with an unearthly light. Then, as suddenly as he appeared, the young man simply vanished.

This was not to be the only time the spirit of the young man would make itself known in that room. Some two years later, another coed who was staying in the room reported that one night, while alone there, she was startled from her studies when the locked door to the room violently sprang open, as though by some powerful unseen force. Later, when checking with her roommates, the girl found that both had witnessed similar incidents.

About two months later, just before Thanksgiving break, the same young woman was in her room standing before her stereo, when she became aware of an intense feeling that she was not alone. As she turned to see who had entered the room, her body passed through an icy cold spot of air immediately behind her that seemed to evaporate immediately. She was alone in the room . . . or so it seemed.

In the proceeding weeks, both of her roommates in turn shared the experience of being alone in the room and feeling a "presence" there. Often these incidents were marked by the sudden occurrence of a cold spot. Finally, one evening the three roommates were together in their room after a long day of classes and studying. As the hour was late, the lights were off and the women were just drifting into sleep when their repose was disturbed by a light that suddenly shot from the closet across the room toward the window. As the women sat up and began to speculate as to the source of the strange light, they were further shocked to hear the unmistakable sound of something heavy falling to the floor from a central table in the room where the stereo was stored. Quickly turning on the light, the young women found the stereo intact and nothing on the floor beside the table. An impish prank, perhaps, perpetrated by their resident apparition.

While the first two spirits said to occupied the third floor of Stevens Hall are of a benign and perhaps frivolous nature, a third specter said to walk the halls is of a more tragic and even pitiable disposition. It is that of a young boy, who has been seen by generations of students.

For many years the story has been handed down that shortly after Stevens Hall was constructed, a young boy was hidden for a time on the third floor of the building. Perhaps he was a runaway from the nearby orphanage, which was known to be a severe and even abusive facility. Perhaps he was simply a wayward youth taken in by kind-hearted students at the time. In truth, since no historical record of his presence exists, no one will ever know his real identity, or even if he did in fact exist.

Nevertheless, in the legend told of him the young boy met a harsh and mysterious fate. Though housed and cared for by the generosity of the students at the time, his presence was of course hidden from the college administration and particularly from the headmistress, a stern woman who lived in an apartment on the first floor of Stevens. If found, the boy would certainly have been sent to less congenial surroundings and the young women who offered him shelter would have faced immediate expulsion.

His presence, however, could not be completely hidden from the campus community and in time rumors of his occupancy on the third floor of Stevens reached the ears of the headmistress. One bitterly cold night that winter, the woman came knocking on the door of the room where the boy was concealed and demanded to search the room. Before opening the door, the young women looked desperately for a place to hide the boy. Since the small room afforded him no real place of hiding, the child, it was said, was coaxed into crawling out onto the window ledge where he was told to stay until told to come in.

However, after searching the room thoroughly without discovering the child, the headmistress was still not satisfied. She ordered the girls to immediately come to her apartment where she would interrogate them further. With no other options open to them, the young women reluctantly followed the headmistress down to her apartment, leaving their charge in his precarious predicament.

The young women were detained to answer questions for over an hour before a warm fire, all the while thinking of the child on the ledge, facing the bitter cold and unable to come back into safety and warmth. Finally they were dismissed by their headmistress and flew up the three flights of stairs to their room. Upon entering, they raced to the window and threw it open.

The boy, however, was gone. Frantically, the girls surveyed the ledge and the ground below, but no token of his presence was found. Panicked, the students rushed downstairs and outside into the snow, but the boy was nowhere to be seen. Further, examination showed that the snow beneath the window was drifted naturally, leaving no signs of the impact of a small body and no tiny footsteps leading away into the night.

It is a strange and evocative story. Of course, several logical and historical flaws become apparent as the story is told, and many may choose to relegate the tale to the realm of historical myth. However, this does not explain the recurrent sightings of a ghostly boy on the third floor of Stevens Hall. His frequent presence has been reported for over a century. It is said that several decades ago a dorm supervisor, checking on students late one night, was puzzled to hear a child's laughter echoing though the empty third floor hallway, followed by the patter of small feet receding into the distance.

A maintenance worker working on the wiring system during summer break in the mid 1960s was reportedly disturbed by repeatedly finding his tools suddenly misplaced. After searching in vain for his missing implements several times, the man was about to leave the area in frustration when he heard the sound of a child playing outside the door to the room where he was working. Knowing he should be alone in the building, the workman walked to the door and into the hallway, only to find it empty. More disturbing still was the fact that as the man stood surveying the empty passage, he found that his missing tools were lying on the floor before him.

However, the actual sightings of the by-now-famous Blue Boy

have garnered the most attention. Time and again, it is said that young women studying alone in their third floor rooms on cold winter nights, when the wind batters the old building, have been distracted by a persistent tapping sound at their window. Investigating the sound, the frightened coeds are said to be confronted with the face of a child peering at them from the other side of the glass, some three stories above the ground. Through the crystalline forms of the frost on the window, his face appears blue, like that of a person in the last stages of hypothermia.

Needless to say, many of the women who have experienced this sighting have reacted with terror and outright hysteria. One young woman, however, seems to have been more inclined to write off the vision as a product of her own imagination. Working at her desk late one bitterly cold night, the woman happened to glance out the window and caught sight of the cadaverous blue face peering in at her. As she watched, wide-eyed, the face disappeared, seeming to float to one side of the window.

Unwilling to believe what she had seen, the coed rubbed her eyes and returned to her work, only to have her eyes drawn to a movement at the window once again. Turning, she again saw the face of a boy peering at her through the frost on the window. Even from across the room she could see that his eyes burned with a pathetic longing, as though in a silent plea for the comfort and peace he had never found.

Now convinced that she was under the sway of some sort of hallucination, the young girl fled her room. After calming her nerves with a soft drink and a walk through the hall, she returned to her room and settled back at her desk.

However, as she resumed her studies, she could not help but glance once more at the window. Gratefully, this time she saw no face there. Instead, scratched across the frost in a childlike hand was the plea:

ƎM ꟼ⅃ƎH

Other ghostly tales are told on campus. The Theta Chi fraternity house on Carlisle Street is said to be inhabited by two ghosts. According to the tales told of the place, one of the spirits is that of a fraternity alumnus who wished to be buried in the basement of the house. When his wish was not honored, strange sounds began to emanate from the house at all hours of the day and night. Footsteps were heard traversing empty halls and rapping noises were heard throughout the home.

The second spirit is supposed to be that of a man named Thompson who, it is claimed, murdered his wife in a basement room while the house was a boarding residence. Eventually, Thompson confessed his guilt to local authorities and, while awaiting justice, hung himself. Ever since, his basement room has been the scene of odd and inexplicable occurrences. Doors open and then slowly shut by themselves, as though an invisible presence were entering the room. Light switches unaccountably flick themselves on and off. Objects have been known to levitate before being pushed off shelves by an unseen hand.

Not to be outdone, the Phi Gamma Delta house on campus is said to have its own resident spirit. This apparition stems from a fire some years ago in which one fraternity member died. Since that time, fraternity members report being awakened in the early hours of the morning by the disembodied cry of "fire!" Quick investigation reveals no fire is present. Others report seeing the misty form of a man in odd corners of the building late at night. As Mark Nesbitt observes, perhaps brotherhood truly is forever.

All throughout the breadth and width of the Gettysburg campus, strange and foreboding forms are said to walk. Where once the battle to end slavery reached its bloody climax, now apparitions might linger, clinging to some semblance of a life that has been denied them. Perhaps they are merely the product of folklore and legend. However, in this now-quiet place of education, it is not so hard to imagine that ghosts do tread with silent steps, reminders of a time when a nation's pain boiled and raged and hell came to Pennsylvania.

Sources

Chapter 1: "The Ghost of College Hall"

Haunted Places: The National Directory, Dennis William Houck. Penguin Books, 1996: 178.

Beneath the Whispering Maples: The History of Simpson College, Joseph W. Walt. Simpson College Press, 1995: 325.

The Simpsonian, 27 October 1994: 10.

The Simpsonian, 31 October 1991: 1.

Firsthand accounts of the death of Mildred Hedges, compiled by Simpson College Archives Department.

Personal interviews, correspondence and research.

Chapter 2: "The Return of the Gipper"

Haunted Indiana, Mark Marimen. Thunder Bay Press, 1997: 20-33.

Notre Dame Observer, 4 March 1983: 8-10.

South Bend Tribune, 11 March 1990: D1.

Firsthand accounts from the University of Notre Dame Archives.

Personal interviews, correspondence and research.

Chapter 3: "The Phantom of the Purple Masque"

Haunted Heartland, Beth Scott and Michael Norman. Stanton and Lee Publishers, 1985: 152-156.

Historic Haunted America, Michael Norman and Beth Scott. Tom Doherty Associates, 1995:167-170.

Manhattan Mercury, 27 October 1985: D1.

Kansas State Collegian, 7 July 1987: 4.

Kansas State Collegian, 3 May 1994, 1.

Manhattan Mercury, 1988 KSU Edition: 8.

Kansas State Collegian, 31 October 1995: 5.

Kansas State Collegian, 31 October 31 1991: 2.
Kansas State Collegian, 27 October 1989: 4.
Kansas State Collegian, Back To School Issue, August 1987: 6E
Kansas State Collegian, 31 October 1978: 12.
Kansas State Collegian, 10 May 1977: 9.
Manhattan Mercury, 28 November 1995: 41.
Kansas State Collegian, 2 November 1995: 3.
Personal interviews, correspondence and research.

Chapter 4: "The Curse of Rafinesque"
Des Moines Tribune, 30 October 1980: 13.
Haunted Heartland, Beth Scott and Michael Norman. Stanton and
    Lee, 1985: 131-134.
Personal interviews, correspondence and research.

Chapter 5: "The Faceless Nun Of Foley Hall"
Haunted Indiana, Mark Marimen. Thunder Bay Press, 1997:
    34-42.
Poem from "Toast to Foley Hall," Rosemary Nudd, SP. (Used with
    permission.)
"The Ghost of Foley Hall," *Indiana Folklore Journal,* Volume 1,
    No. 2, 1975: 117-123.
The Woods, October 1975.
Personal interviews, correspondence and research.

Chapter 6: "The Spectral Cadet of West Point"
Press Release, U.S. Military Academy, December 1972, U.S. Mili-
    tary Academy Archives.
Haunted Places: The National Directory, Dennis William Houck.
    Penguin Books, 1996: 309.
Newburgh Evening News, 22 November 1972: 1A.
Hudson Valley, July 1988: 81.
Philadelphia Enquirer, 3 December 1972.
Time, 4 December 1972.
The Assembly (West Point cadet newspaper), March 1973.
The Assembly, January 1990: 28.
White Plains Reporter Dispatch, 29 November 1972: 1A.

Times Herald Record, 16 November 1972: 3A.
Sunday Record, 26 November 1972: 11.
New York Times, 21 November 1972: 45.
Personal interviews, correspondence and research.

Chapter 7: "The Ghosts of William and Mary"
The Ghosts of Virginia Volume III, L. B. Taylor. Progress Printing,
    1996: 355-362.
The Ghosts Williamsburg, L. B. Taylor. Progress Printing, 1983.
The Ghosts of Tidewater, L. B. Taylor. Progress Printing, 1989.
Haunted Places: The National Directory, Dennis William Houck.
    Penguin Books, 1996: 438.
A Galaxy of Ghosts, Jane Polonsky and Joan Drum. Polydrum
    Publications: 33.
The Flat Hat, (student newspaper), 1 November 1985, 15.
The Flat Hat, 31 October 1975: 1.
The Flat Hat, 5 March 1971: 5.
Personal interviews, correspondence and research.

Chapter 8: "Millikin's Ghosts"
Haunted Decatur Book 3: Ghosts of Millikin, Troy Taylor: 1996.
Personal interviews, correspondence and research.

Chapter 9:
"The Troubled Spirits of Marquette University"
Marquette Tribune, 26 October 1995: 11.
Marquette Tribune, 31 October 1991: 5.
Personal interviews, correspondence and research.

Chapter 10: "The Guardian Spirit of Clet Hall"
Personal interviews, correspondence and research.

Chapter 11: "The Ghosts of Kenyon College"
Haunted Ohio, Chris Woodyard. Kestrel Publications, 1991:
    137-142.
"Shades of Purple: The Ghosts of Kenyon College," unpublished
    manuscript by Heather S. Frost. Kenyon College Archives
    Deptartment.

Cleveland Plain Dealer, 1 April 1979: 6.

Columbus Dispatch, 30 March 1979: 15.

Unpublished manuscript by Mary Melber. Kenyon College Archives Department.

Kenyon Collegian, 15 April 1993: 8.

Kenyon Collegian, 31 October 1988: 4.

Kenyon Collegian, 31 October 1991.

Kenyon Collegian, 28 September 1995: 5.

Kenyon Collegian, 27 October 1994: 8-9.

Kenyon Alumni Bulletin, Spring 1979: 4.

Personal interviews, correspondence and research.

Chapter 12: "When Hell Came to Pennsylvania"

Ghosts of Gettysburg, Mark Nesbitt. Thomas Publications, 1991: 34-39, 540-558, 76-79.

Personal interviews, correspondence and research.

Coming Soon . . .

School Spirits Volume 2:
College Ghost Stories of the South and West

Mark Marimen is currently collecting more college ghost stories. If you would like to share a college ghost story, please contact him at at P.O. Box 837, Crown Point, Indiana, 46307, or e-mail him at hhproj@juno.com.